MW01243075

LULLABY
OF THE
SWORD
THE BLADE'S OPUS | BOOK ONE

NIKI TRENTO

Cover by Kismet New Moon Covers

Editing by Niki Trento

Proofreading by Mel Wright

1st Edition

Contents

To Betty White, Bob Saget, and Meat Loaf.
Thank you for the years of laughs, love, and music.

Trigger Warning

This book is for mature readers. Please be aware that there is talk of potentially triggering topics within this book with references to sensitive topics that some readers may find offensive. There are mentions–but not details.

Author's Note

M ODERN MAN BELIEVES IN Heaven and Hell. A simple matter of good vs evil. While there is nothing wrong with that mentality, there is always something more if you look deeper.

The ancient Greeks believed in a different system. The Underworld, Mount Olympus, and the Gods and Goddesses who sat on high. They believed in Titans and Hydras, Pegasus and Cerberus. They believed in the Underworld and all of its domains, including Elysium, Tartarus, and of course, the five rivers.

It is the latter that this tale leans towards. Styx knows she's a demon, and she has a very basic understanding of the Underworld, but she has grown up in the human world. That being said, it is common for her to refer to the Underworld as Hell.

I suppose when the day is done, there really isn't any right or wrong answer for what you believe in. As long as you strive to be the best that you can be. Be you angel, demon, or something in between, we are all here for a reason. It just so happens that Styx's reason is a part of the destiny that she must fulfill.

Disclaimer My version of Styx is NOT the story of the Goddess Styx as she is known in Greek Mythology.

Chapter One

Styx

"N Not again!" I cry out in disbelief. "Every single fucking time..." Leaving my complaints unspoken—no one to hear them anyway—I crawl out from under the blankets. I know it isn't every time, but it sure feels that way. As soon as my head hits the pillow, that familiar and unwanted tingle races through my body like a shockwave. I just want one night this week. One. One night to not have to go chasing them down.

With one hand, I gently pull my sword from its wall-mounted sheath as I stand. On sore feet, I gingerly step to my dresser. Lifting my necklace from its perch, I slip the thick chain over my head, letting the crucifix rest against my abdomen. The strength of the calling tells me I don't have time to change into my leathers, shame. Let's hope my belly shirt doesn't slip up too far, revealing my tits. That would be unprofessional.

Racing through my measly apartment, I snag my hooded cloak from beside the door. It nearly gets caught on the knob as I rush to close the lightweight wood behind me.

As I leave the apartment in a rush, my cloak gripped tightly in my hand, the cross taps against my belly. The heavy chain is snug between my breasts.

I hate the hunting. I hate this tingling feeling that notifies me every single time there's one nearby. I don't want to be the hunter. I also do not want to be the hunted.

The city streets are dark, not a single streetlamp casts their soft glow against the pavement. Not on these side streets, beyond the hustle and bustle of downtown. Not even a car, with too bright headlights, driving too fast on these residential streets. But it doesn't matter. I can see into the darkness. Part of the beast that lives within me. One of the few things the crucifix cannot stop.

The silver-plated crucifix hanging between my tits is not a religious insignia. No, it's a protection. A protection for myself and for others. As long as they aren't what I am hunting. The cold metal brushes against my heated skin as I run through the streets, determined to find the source that's causing my brain and body to tingle with warning.

Somewhere close by, I can feel it pulling me like a magnet. One of them is out there. One of them is going against their code. Against the agreements made. Against the laws placed to keep the humans safe.

As if it were a beacon, its scent calls to me. Pulls me.

To the left. Around the corner and behind that building. And there it is, snarling. Foaming at the mouth. I wonder if it's a rogue. Kicked from its society? Banished from its pack? From its family?

Was it like me?

The human pressed against the wall is limp. Her eyes—unseeing—pointed heavenward. Red lips hang open in a silent scream of horror. I wonder if she is internally begging. Begging for peace. Begging for someone to help her as the beast snarls, drool from his sharp teeth dripping on her exposed breasts. Its claws wrapped around her neck.

I can tell she's still alive. Her heartbeat, although slower than it should be, patters on. I can smell her fear. She knows something is wrong, but I wonder if she's in the throes of the magic the beast holds over her. I wonder if she knows just exactly what kind of danger she's in right now. How close she is to becoming one of them. How close she is to becoming the next target skewered by my sword.

All of this registers in my mind within the blink of an eye. Just as my plan of attack does. As if time for the beast and the human has slowed to a snail's pace. For me it whirls by in an instant. With my next breath, I am behind him, my blade against his neck.

"Are you serious right now?" I growl. "You do realize that you're breaking about a hundred different codes, yeah?" I begin to tick them off as my blade hovers just below what would be an Adam's Apple on a human male. "Within the city limits. With a human female? One who," *Sniff, sniff.* "As I thought...is a virgin. Are you looking for her soul, or are you just feeding some other kind of need?"

The beast snarls. Frozen and afraid of the copper and silver sword resting against its throat. They are all afraid of Tod, my sword. Alone, these metals can mortally wound, bound together—as they are—means an excruciating death.

"Release her mind, demon," I command. The authority in my quiet voice is as solid and terrifying as Tod's blade. It even gives me goosebumps.

"Don't have it," he grumbles. His teeth gnash together, adding clicks to his words.

"Dude! I know you have her under your thrall. I wasn't hatched yesterday, ya know." I press Tod into the leathery skin of the demon's throat. "Do you really think you have the upper hand here? Let. Her. Go." My voice doesn't waver, my hand doesn't so much as tremble. Some of these demons really think they are stronger than me and scarier than my blade. Idjits.

Just as I hear the sharp hiss of blood hitting my blade, the female human's teeth crash together with a loud click. I peek at her from the corner of my eye as her chin lowers, her eyes blinking rapidly. She's coming out of the thrall. Before she has a chance to register the demon in front of her, I punch her in the temple. She falls limp, but this time is unconscious, safe from the demon.

Movement from the demon catches my attention. I know without looking that it thinks it can get away from me. Unfortunately for him, I don't need to swing in order to sever his head, only a little pressure. Before he can take a full step away, Tod slips through the leathery skin and corded muscles like a hot knife to butter. The demon's blood sizzles and pops on the copper and silver before the blade seems to drink it up. An appreciative groan blooms in my mind. For now, Tod is satiated.

Chapter Two

Styx

WITH THE ASHES OF the demon now floating on the wind, I take the time to really look at the human. She must be quite weak for such a low-level demon to have gotten the drop on her. He couldn't even glamour himself, so he must have been quick.

She needs healing. That phantom voice hums in my head.

"No shit. Tell me something I don't know," I grumble. Kneeling at her side, I place my palm on the flat of Tod's blade, easing the cool metal against the human's neck. A humming—a song of some sort—vibrates through my hand before traveling up my arm. The process is as familiar to me as breathing. Tod is soaking up any toxins that may have seeped into the punctures the demon made with his gnarled teeth. Once that is done, the song changes slightly and the broken skin begins to knit itself back together perfectly. Not a red spot of irritation or a scar in sight.

From what I have witnessed in the past, when the sword heals, it must also wipe the memory from the human. They tend to just stand up and walk blindly to wherever they think they should be as if nothing happened to them at all.

Now, I don't know what gives my sword the ability to heal humans, but I have done some experimenting. Through those experiments, I've determined that the sword only heals humans who are injured—no matter to what degree, save death—by demons. It can't heal a scraped knee or a busted nose from a bar fight. Or at least, it doesn't *choose* to heal those things.

The humming stops suddenly, the annoying ringing of silence takes its place. I back away from the female and slink into the shadows. Just as all the others have, the female stands up and dusts herself off. Her hands tug at her skirt, straightening it. With my advanced sight, I can see the glassy look of her eyes. She has no idea what she is doing right now. And then, she walks away, carrying on with her life as if she wasn't a hair's breadth away from becoming a corpse...or worse, a demon.

"Do you think I can actually get some sleep now? It's only been—I don't know—four days?" I snark at Tod as I return it to the leather scabbard on my back.

Three days, the voice responds.

"But who's counting, right? Asshole. Next time you call me, I'm ignoring you." I know I'm lying, there's no way I could let a human suffer just so I can get some sleep. I'm sure the sword knows it, too.

As quickly as I had raced to the human's aid, I returned to my humble abode. Being careful to slow down as I reach where others may see me, I make my way up the two flights of stairs before opening my door. I never lock it when I leave, there's no point. The only things I have of any value are my crucifix and my sword, and I never leave home without either one.

I hang my hooded cloak back on the smooth knob-like hook next to the door, flipping the lock now that I'm home. I'm not sure if anyone pays much attention to me, but I don't want to risk them coming in while I am in my—hopefully—comatose like sleep. Forgoing a shower, as it would more than likely wake me up, I bypass the bathroom door and step into my bedroom. The crucifix is put back on its stand and Tod is returned to the wall mount. I don't remember my head hitting the pillow before darkness consumes me.

Chapter Three

Unknown

*T*HIS CRAZY FEMALE IS *as mercurial as they come. Which, for her kind, is quite a unique temperament. Demons are lust-filled, insatiable, and crude. But not this one. She has heart, that's what makes her different. While it isn't uncommon for demons to kill each other over the most mundane and trivial matters, she only kills to protect the human race. This, and this alone, is why I chose her to do my bidding.*

Chapter Four

Styx

T HE SUNLIGHT SLITHERS PAST the blackout curtain's edge and pierces through my eyelids. Fucking sun.

I roll over and look at the beaten clock on the crate next to my bed. Ten after six. Good, I got more than an hour of sleep. Thank you, Nyx. What is today? Thursday? Friday?

Saturday, by your calendar. Echoes in my head. That voice, it can be helpful, but sometimes I wish she/he/it would just shut the hell up!

"Shit! I have to go to work today!" I scramble out of my lumpy bed and race to the bathroom, yanking my crop top over my head and dropping it somewhere on the floor. As I shimmy out of my shorts, I turn on the hot water full blast. It takes a few minutes to actually heat up, but once it does, it's like hellfire on my skin. Blessed heat!

Saturday evenings are the best time to soak in all this glorious hot water. However, I have a schedule to keep, so I rush through my process.

I've been lucky to snag a job and I don't want to lose it. Jobs are something that demons usually don't worry about. Not that they would be able to, what with their grotesque features and desire to devour souls and such. So, yeah, not a normal demon thing to do at all. Instead, they tend to just steal whatever the fuck they want.

Luckily for me, I don't look anything like a demon...just in the eyes, but contacts help with that. Side note...to cover red eyes, go dark. I don't mean red like I've been out drinking all night; I mean red irises. Bright, blood red. It took a lot of trial and error trying to find the right contacts without having to go see some eye doctor and have them out me as a demon. Thank the Goddess Nyx for online shopping!

Rinsing the last of the conditioner from my dark brown hair, I give it a good twisting to expel as much water from it as I can. I run my hands quickly down my legs like a squeegee before stepping out of the old, clawfoot tub. Stepping onto the white bathmat, I giggle to myself as my wet feet leave blood red marks. The novelty bathmat never gets old.

Focus. Clock's a-tickin'!

"Oh, stuff it. I have plenty of time!" I argue with the voice in my head. I'd call it my fairy godfather, but I don't think demons have those. Maybe he is just a result of my psychosis? I mean, I'm a demon girl living in a human world, there has to be some side effect to that, right? Regardless of what the voice is—and the fact that I love to argue with it—I speed up my drying and stalk out to the small dresser to grab my work clothes and underwear.

It's Saturday, one of the busiest nights. It's also the night that Kenny and Eddie always show up. With my hair wrapped in a towel, I fight with my decision about what to wear. Eddie likes me in blue, but Kenny prefers red. "I really need to get some blended colors," I say out loud. If they didn't tip so fucking well, I wouldn't give two shits what I wore. Black and sexy is enough by my standards.

Why not your blue lace bra and the red thong? Satisfy both cretins in one go.

"Good point. They *are* the same style..." I can't believe I just agreed with my other personality. Mark it on the calendar, it won't happen again. Pulling the mixed set out of the drawer, I shimmy my curvy ass into the thong first. Then, I slip my arms into the straps and fasten the eye hooks. Bending over, I wiggle my chest while holding the double D cups, allowing my tits to rest naturally and completely inside. This style of bra is my favorite, it has cushions on the inside that literally look like hands that act as extra support to push the twins up and together, creating the delicious cleavage that gets those boys drooling.

Most of the girls leave outfits at the club and waltz in there looking like something you'd find sleeping behind a dumpster. Not me. I gear up before I leave. I don't have a lot of in the way of furniture, and I live in one of the absolute worst apartment buildings in the area...but my clothes? Those are my life. Literally, without the lace, spandex, and leather, I wouldn't make as much money as I do. Hmm...lace and leather, sounds perfect!

To cover the bra and thong, I pull on a black lacy top that has more openings than thread, and tearaway black leather hotpants. Had I been going out to party, I would have bothered with some fishnets, but stripping those off is a pain in the devil's ass. Before selecting my stilettos, I go back to the bathroom to do my makeup and put in my contacts.

The towel wrapped around my hair is soaked through now. Shit, I really need to buy another one, this one barely does the job anymore. I should have listened to my other personality and bought more than one to begin with. Oh well. Live and learn. I take the towel off and do my best to dry my hair. Maybe I should invest in a blow dryer.

As I finish getting ready, I can't help but sing to myself. "I'm a demon girl...in a human wo-orld...Come on, Demon, let's go party...Ah Ah Ah Yeah..."

Twenty minutes later, my makeup is done to perfection, my hair is styled just right, and my contacts are in place. I look just like any other human. If that human happened to be a high-class stripper, I guess.

"Frankie! What did I tell you about wearing my costumes!?" I hear Jazz scream before I even open the back door of the club. Seems like every week those two are going at it over some piece of clothing or another.

"A set of gloves, Jazz. Shit, my hands are smaller than yours, I didn't stretch them!"

"Buy your own shit!"

"Girls! Enough! Customers are going to be coming in soon and I can hear your catfight out in the lobby." That voice belongs to Feather. She started out as a stripper back in the day. Now, though, she owns the place. Of all the clubs I've gone to looking for work, The French Tickler is the cleanest—and I mean that about the girls themselves, too—by far. Feather has the girls—except me—tested regularly and has amazing health coverage.

How do I get around that? Easy, Feather knows what I am. All of what I am. That's one of the reasons she hired me, actually. She never explained the whole thing to me, but she has demonic connections—or did at some point—and she took me under her proverbial wing.

Because of my ability to kick ass, even without Tod, Feather has me work as a bouncer, too. The regulars love it because they actually get to talk to me. The other girls refuse to get all social with these men unless they are getting paid to do it. I find it refreshing. I guess in a way it reminds me of who I am. The men in all their perversions keep me grounded. Once you get beyond the sexual innuendo and advances, most of them are really not bad men. Don't get me wrong, there are some that pop in now and again that set even my blood to boil. I keep a close eye on those monsters. I expect to catch a whiff of brimstone or sulfur one of these days.

I walk into the dressing room that is conveniently located by the back door. These girls have become my friends...well, my work-friends. I've never gone out drinking with them, nor have I ever invited any of them over to my place, but I get along with most of them.

"Whaddup, Styx?" Skyla greets as she spots me in the reflection of the mirror she is sitting at. One of her eyes is a menage of colors, the other looking like its drab twin. "Damn, girl! I wish I had your talent for makeup, you look smokin'!" Skyla whirls around in her seat before stepping over to me. She studies my red and blue eyeshadow with the scrutiny of a tax auditor. Her smooth caramel skin is so dark compared to my almost pale complexion. "Lessons. Seriously, I will pay you!"

Chuckling nervously at the implications of that, I say, "Your makeup looks amazing...when it's complete." I nod towards her unfinished eye, causing a braying laugh to erupt past her plump, red lips.

"Best get a move on. Don't need Feather hollerin' at me for holding up the show." Skyla gives me a quick one-armed hug before returning to her makeup station.

"What's the lineup tonight?" I ask, setting my small bag in my assigned locker, spinning the dial on the cheap gym room lock.

"Skyla, Jazz, Nova, me, then Korra. You've got the door tonight," Frankie tells me.

Damn. Not that I mind covering the door, but normally Feather will give me a heads up so I know to wear something I can easily fight in. Good thing I tend to wear hotpants more often than not. But it's also a headspace thing. Kind of like when you are prepared to go dancing with the girls but end up sitting at a hot wing bar with the guys instead. Totally different headspace.

"Feather must've forgotten to tell you. Nova has some car payment and needs to work tonight. You are the only one that can pull double duties," Frankie explains, disdain dripping from her words. Frankie and Jazz may argue like sisters, but she and Nova do *not* get along. Actually, none of the girls like Nova.

"No worries here. I don't mind being out on the floor." I look around at the gals and see that Nova isn't even here. I'm sure she will show up two minutes before her time.

Liar.

Bite me, I mentally snap.

"I'd better get to the door. You gals need anything?" I ask while carefully unclasping the chain of my crucifix. The metal chills me as I wrap it around my neck, making the cross rest above my cleavage. The arrowhead point brings more attention to my cleavage. I can fight with it long or short, but at the door, I prefer it closer to my body. Asshole drunks tend to think they can use it to choke me out.

"I'm good, Sugar," Skyla says as she finishes her makeup. Jazz, Frankie, and Korra all give me a thumbs up.

"Remember...if they get too handsy..."

"Yes, Styx, we know. Slap the thigh twice and you'll take care of it." Korra teases, sounding like a petulant child who has heard Mom's warning about a dozen times too many.

Shaking my head, I turn towards the main pit of the club. "Good luck, bitches!" It's our way of saying break a leg. Giggles follow me through the door.

Chapter Five

Styx

T HE NIGHT IS HALF over with. Nova still hasn't shown for her set, which is coming up soon. If she were any of the other girls, I'd be worried by now. As it is...

"Styx! Baby! How the hell are you?" Kenny bellows as he walks through the door. My regulars know that I usually wrap up the show, so they tend to come in late.

"Better now that you're here," I coo. Flirting, now that is something I am almost as good at as fighting.

"Be still my heart. Why aren't you dancing tonight?" Kenny asks.

Snorting through my nose I say, "Nova has a car payment due."

"Car payment...is that what they are calling it now?" Kenny asks, shaking his head.

I raise an eyebrow, tilt my head, and cross my arms over my chest. Silently asking him to explain.

Kenny taps the side of his nose as a quick, overexaggerated sniff makes his nostrils flare. "Nova has an...extra-curricular hobby, if you know what I mean." He's talking about coke. Who the hell does coke anymore?

I nod as my lip finds its way between my teeth. I wonder if Feather is aware of Nova's problem. Doubtful. There is no way Feather would keep her employed if she were on drugs. Like I said, The French Tickler is the cleanest club, right down to what's between the girls' thighs.

"Don't sweat it, Styx. She's a big girl." He has mistaken my silence for worry over the cokehead.

"And...forgotten. Are you going to stay for the rest of the show?" I ask as I check the I.D. of another male, letting him pass.

"Only if you let me buy you a drink." Kenny winks at me. It's always the same line. It has become a bit of an inside joke. I always tell him he's on, but I never take his offer. He moves to the table closest to the door, the one he always occupies when I'm not on the stage.

One of the waitresses, a new one I've never seen before, brings a menu over to Kenny just as Eddie joins him. He must have slipped in before I got to the door. Odd. With their order taken, she moves back to the bar.

A few more men enter the club, some are half drunk already. I make a mental note to keep my eye on them. I still haven't seen Nova. I look at the clock above the bar, three minutes until she is to start. Jazz is on the stage strutting her stuff.

Another benefit of being on the door, I get to watch the other girls. Not that they do it for me sexually, but it's interesting to watch how their bodies move to the music. Jazz does a backbend, lifting her long legs to wrap around the pole fixed to the center of the stage. There are three altogether, but she always uses the center one. Using her core muscles, she pulls her torso up from the floor and grabs the pole with her hands. Her ability to move in a way that looks like she is floating is a real crowd pleaser. Other than myself, she is the only one that can do that.

"Styx," Feather says from behind me. "Nova still isn't here. If she doesn't show by the time Jazz is finished, I'm moving Frankie up. Will you close us out?"

"Of course. What about the door?"

"Jeremy can take it. I need you up there." Feather doesn't show signs of concern or worry, just that she has an obligation to the patrons to give them a good show. She actually makes the girls switch up their routines each time they go on. Something fresh. Always.

As if he heard her say his name, Jeremy lumbers over to the door. He is the kind of guy who doesn't say much, wears shirts that are way too tight, but accentuates his muscles. And his muscles' muscles. His floppy blonde hair and piercing blue eyes make him look both like the boy next door, and the boy your mother warned you about. He nods and I return the gesture, weaving my way through the tables to go backstage.

Jazz's song ends, and I check my makeup in the mirror by the stage entrance. Perfect. I roll my shoulders and wait for her to come down the three steps.

Just then, tingles vibrate through me, rocking me to my core. "Not now!" I screech as I dig my nails into my palms.

Move it! Now!

"Fuck! Jazz...go back out there. I'll give you a hundred bucks! PLEASE!" I beg her.

Startled and confused, and looking like a deer caught in headlights, Jazz nods before backing up onto the stage.

"Fucking pieces of crusted cum!" I curse and complain as I instinctively hunt down the demon. "Sweaty ball-sucking morons!"

Tell me how you really feel.

"Don't get me started on you, you spunkless twat licker!" Thank the goddess it is so late, and most people are home, at a bar, or too drunk to realize I am blurring past them while shouting obscenities.

As I close in on the foul stench of sulfur, I pull Tod from the sheath strapped to my back. How no one noticed it is beyond me, but now isn't the time to worry about it.

A flash of bright red hair suddenly pops up in front of the demon. Over his shoulder, I see her wiping the corner of her lip with her middle finger before sticking it in her mouth. I know that face. What the fuck is Nova doing with a rancid demon?

Sucking his chode by the looks of it.

Classy. And eww!

Zipping my blade between the two, I have it resting nicely against the demon's throat.

"Woah! Down, girl! If this one is yours..." Nova begins, hands up as she backs away. "Styx?"

"You are late for work." Of all the clever things I could have said. Denying the demon as mine in some over exaggerated puking manner, I tell her she's late. Way to drop the ball on that one, Styx.

"Yeah—well...Margan says I don't have to go back to that club. He's going to take care of me." Nova wraps her hands around the demon's arm, the perfect image of an infatuated schoolgirl.

"Yeah. Take care of you. Right. Margan, is it? Does she know who you really are?" Adding pressure to his neck as I watch Nova's eyes. They are a bit glassy, which means she is seeing his glamour. "Drop the glam, Margan. Let Nova see the *man* you really are."

"Drop your blade. I have no idea what you are talking about," he sneers.

"Really? Hmm. If that's the case and I'm wrong about you...then sucking some of the blood from your throat with my blade shouldn't bother you. Right?" I apply more pressure.

"What is she...Styx...what are you..." Her eyes widen as I assume his glamour fades away. A small giggle blips between her lips, slowly turning into a hysterical hyena's cackle.

She's gone looney. The voice...my alter ego...my other personality...sighs in my head.

The demon joins in, his grotesque breath clouds the surrounding air. His laughter is more sinister than Nova's crazy one. The sound reminds me of phlegm stuck at the back of a throat, wet and thick. I suppress a gag at the sound of it.

"You didn't even have her in a thrall?!" I screech, realizing he didn't bother to ease her from handsome man to vile demon. Before he could answer or suck in a breath, Tod is slicing through his neck, decapitating the foul beast. Once again, the blood sizzles before it disappears into the glowing copper and silver blade. The familiar groan of pleasure following close behind echoes in my mind as if I'd made the sound myself. I suppose if that phantom voice is my personality, I guess in a way it was me.

Nicely done. Now, deal with her.

"This isn't my first rodeo, fucktard." My gaze lands on Nova, a single drop of the demon's blood is snaking a trail from the bridge of her nose, around her nostril, and towards her upper lip. "Fuck!" I grab her chin, her raucous laughter simmers to a nervous giggle as I lay the tip of my sword below the quickly descending drip. Like magic, the blood and the rash that was undoubtedly under it, are gone.

Nova continues to giggle, her eyes wide and unfocused, she looks at me without really seeing me.

"What the fuck am I supposed to do about you?" I click my tongue against the roof of my mouth. "Will the sword be able to heal crazy?" I muse aloud.

It was caused by the demon. Have faith and it will work.

"Well then, here goes nothing." I rest the blade at her temple. Makes sense, right?

After a few tense minutes, Nova stops giggling. She pulls the shoulder of her shirt back up, turns, and walks towards the club. Guess it worked. Nova will be none the wiser that just ten minutes ago, she was sucking down—SHIT!

"How do I know if the sword took that out, too? I mean...what can demon spunk do to a human?" I wait for that phantom voice to respond like it normally does. When silence is the only response I get, I panic.

Nova may be a cum guzzling gutter slut, but she doesn't deserve whatever could happen to her. What if it is like rotting her insides or something?

She'll be fine. You should get back to work.

Not wanting to dwell on the what-ifs, I blur through the alleys and dark city streets towards The French Tickler.

"She was doing what??" Feather paces the length of her office. She and I are the only ones left in the building now. I don't bother repeating myself because I know she is just trying to wrap her mind around this. "And the sword...it took it all? Are you sure?"

I shrug my shoulders. "I think so. What—do you know what could happen to her if there are any traces still left?" Nyx, please let her have an answer.

"She'd be pregnant." Solid, no bullshit answer. No room for argument. Stone. Cold. Fact.

Maybe she misheard me. "She swallowed..."

"Demon seed. Yup. It doesn't have to go in through the cunt, as long as it gets inside the host. And when I say host, that is exactly what she would be. Nova wouldn't be a mother nurturing a baby, she'd be a shell carrying a demon. I can't believe you don't know how demons procreate." Shaking her head, Feather lights a cigarette. She doesn't smoke it, just waves it around as she thinks and paces.

"It isn't like I grew up in Hell surrounded by demons," I state. I've told her this before. I've been to Hell less than a handful of times in my life, none of which were demon biology classes.

"I know. I know. I just—" My boss and confidante stops speaking and lifts her cell phone from her desk. With fingers flying, she taps something out on the glass screen before putting the small device to her ear. "I need to speak with Cooke." A pause. "Cooke. I need your expertise. Yes, just me and Styx. Five minutes."

"Who's Cooke?"

"My demon contact. Out to the bar. He is going to want some drinks waiting for him if he is going to answer some questions."

Just as we finish mixing a slew of drinks and setting them all on the bar, the strong scent of brimstone tickles my nose. At the edge of my vision, a deep red plume of smoke swirls into nothingness. I turn and come face to face with the most un-demon-like demon I have ever seen.

Despite the brimstone and smoke, the creature that stands before me is broad in the shoulders, trim in the waist, and has thighs that can crack a walnut—or a skull. Bringing my eyes from his large converse—wink, wink—to his stern chin, chiseled jaw, and blazing red eyes. The eyes are the only part of him that even hints at his demonhood.

"Styx, meet Cooke. Or how he is more commonly known, Charon," Feather states in a very uncharacteristic swoony kind of way.

It takes me a second for the realization to hit me, and it happens like a few pounds of torbernite. "Charon? As in *the* Charon?" Can I just take a minute to fangirl over here? The demon is well known across all worlds for running his ferry over the Rivers Acheron and Styx. I always felt it was quite the honor to be named after one of the most famous rivers in Hell. Even if I have no real idea who gave me the name.

"It is lovely to put a face to the demon I've heard so much about over the years," Charon tips his head on a slight diagonal, his perfectly groomed, dark hair misbehaves for a moment as it slips over one fiery eye. My confusion must show on my face as he continues, "Feather has told me much about you, Styx." Charon leans in all conspiratorial-like and stage whispers, "It has always been my favorite of the two rivers."

Woah! Is Charon flirting with me? No. That can't be right. He's a demon. Demons only flirt when they are attempting to feed.

While I stammer over some nonsensical response, I realize that Charon isn't wearing an illusion. There is no glamour hiding grotesque fangs and horrific malformations. He...he is like me.

"She is in desperate need of an education on demonology, Charon. I was hoping you'd be able to help her." Feather fiddles with a strand of her blonde hair that is curled just above her cleavage. For a woman of her age, she doesn't look much older than any of the girls she has working for her. I wonder if that has anything to do with her connection to Charon.

"I suppose it is about time she learns some hard truths, huh? You've been on this side of the inferno for how long now?"

"Oh, umm." Shrugging my shoulders, I tell him, "Since I was about three human years, I believe."

"You must be joking!" he scoffs. "They let you leave at quite the young age. That...that is just preposterous!" The flames in Charon's eyes seem to burn brighter by a few degrees as he looks between me and Feather.

"No, sir. I-I-I was..." What was I? I don't remember having parents, foster or otherwise. I don't remember anyone stowing me away on some grand mission like you read about in paranormal romance novels. I just...was.

"Interesting." Charon steps closer to me—which doesn't take much as he hasn't moved far from me since he smoked in. His red eyes seem to bore into mine. Dark brows arrow towards his nose before shooting up in surprise. The pinpricks that were his pupils are now enlarged, leaving the barest trace of his ruby irises.

"What do you see?" I hear Feather ask, seemingly farther away than I remember her being.

Flashes of somebody in a thick black robe carrying a small package of sorts spark to life in my mind. The robed figure's head swings back and forth as if waiting for something to jump out at it. I can almost taste the nervousness from it as it moves quickly from the shore and onto a boat that lies hidden by crags of torbernite.

The figure steps quickly—perhaps too quickly, judging by how it almost falls into the river—onto the small boat. The black and green glow tells me the water is that of the River Styx, the River of Hate. Placing its package on the bottom of the ferry boat, then pushing from the banks with a large, crooked stick, the figure searches its surroundings once more.

"It can't be." The words leave Charon's mouth in a disbelieving whisper.

Chapter Six

Styx

AS ONE OF THE most prominent demons Hell has to offer breathes out his words, a chill slithers up my spine. Whatever it is he is doing to me is bringing odd images to the forefront of my mind. I can only assume that he is doing some kind of mind reading mumbo jumbo. Part of me relishes in the privilege that someone as great as Charon is using such a precious gift on me. The other part of me is terrified at what all these, now jumbled, images mean.

The green stones of the torbernite—aka the mineral of Hell—and the blasts of fire pits give way to the churning river before being traded for a place I recognize as a city. Tall buildings, a looming suspension bridge I know as the George Washington, and cars. Lots and lots of cars.

The hooded figure pulls the boat under the GW, hiding it in the shadow of the near century old bridge. It removes the heavy cloak, revealing jeans, a dark sweater, and...billowy brown hair. A woman. A *human* woman. Well, at least she *looks* human. Charon and I are living proof that looks can be quite deceiving.

Charon could be seeing my future for all I know. What would I be smuggling from Hell? Because that is exactly what the woman was doing. Or will do? Is doing? I suck at tenses.

Anyway, I want to ask him, but would that be considered rude?

Ask him. You have a right to know.

"Right," I say aloud before realizing. "What does it mean?" I ask, trying to pretend I wasn't talking to myself.

"Sorry?" Charon's eyes instantly clear, his focus returning to the here and now.

"The images. The cloaked figure...the woman?"

"Wait. You saw that?" Charon's eyebrows inch closer to his hairline in surprise. Now I'm nervous. Was I not supposed to see that? Not that I could have kept it from happening. "What did you see?" he asks.

I tell him and Feather about the images that flashed in front of me. Getting a bit less fangirly and a lot more irritated as the two of them keep exchanging glances as I speak. By the time I'm done recounting the visions, my voice has deepened to an angry growl.

"I didn't try to invade your mind or anything, if that is what you're thinking," I snap when neither of them says anything.

"No one has ever—and I have lived more than my share of centuries—been able to sense, let alone *see,* what I was doing." Charon's voice is thick with awe.

"I would say I was sorry if it was something I could control. But seeing as it was a bombardment of imagery that I wasn't even expecting..." I look at Feather, her eyes have gone wide. I assume because of the blunt way I am speaking to a revered demon like Charon. I shrug my shoulders and turn back to the demon.

"On the contrary, I am fascinated, and to be quite honest, intrigued." Charon taps his chin with one long finger. "I would like to delve into this thoroughly," he says, motioning between the two of us. "Until then, would you allow me to try something?"

It's my turn to cock a brow. My hand goes to my crucifix out of habit, caressing the always cool metal. "And what would that be?"

"Trust me?" he asks.

Feather sucks in a breath, causing my gaze to shoot to her. I can't read the expression on her face, though. Has Charon asked her to trust him too? Is that how he locks in a deal?

Unsure for the first time since he smoked in, I bite my lip, an oddly human habit I picked up. Should I trust a demon—of all beings—to do something without explanation? Silently, I pray to Nyx...Guide me in the right direction.

And then I laugh at myself. Out loud. I am literally praying to Charon's mother!

Chapter Seven

Styx

"Tell me something, Mighty Charon, why should I trust you? You are a demon, and demons are not known for being trustworthy." I pop a hip out to the side, making my body look more relaxed than I really am. Inside, my nerves are fidgeting, live wires waiting to be struck down for insubordination.

"Styx!" Feather screeches her admonishment. "How dare you speak to him like that?!"

"It's okay, love. She is completely within her right to be suspicious of me. Demons don't normally work on the side of good. Not unless it serves our own needs and desires." Turning to me, Charon's ruby eyes twinkle with a lightness I would never expect to see on a demon. There's an emotion there that I can't quite put my finger on. "Ask and you shall receive."

"You can tell me anything I want to know? The winning lottery numbers? What is the meaning of life? Who's on first?" Hysterical? Me? Nah! Not in the slightest.

"7-18-21-31-40. For a human? Love and evolving. Yes." Charon smirks as he pulls the Abbott to my Costello, seeming quite proud of himself.

"Cute. So, Charon's a comedian." Shaking my head, fighting a smirk of my own. The fangirling is back...a little. I tamp the bitch down, though. "Explain to me who the woman in the robe is. Was. Will be?"

"There is much you need to know, but that...I'm not sure if you are ready for that one yet." Charon steps back for the first time since our conversation started. Stepping first to the right and then to the left, pacing in front of me, he taps his finger against his dimpled chin. "What I *can* tell you is that demons don't just take random souls. There's a list." He pauses in his rant as if waiting for me to ask him to continue.

I take the bait. "A list?" I urge.

"You know how Reapers work, yes?" At my nod, he continues, "They are given a list of where to be and when. Souls that are about to be available to them to bring to whichever afterlife they are destined for. Demons have their own lists, depending, of course, on their level of power. The one you hunted down tonight and the one before it? They were working off the grid."

"Oka-ay? Obviously, you don't want to answer questions that have anything to do with what I saw or, or about me. Riddle me this, then...Nova. Feather is under the assumption that she could be carrying demon spawn even though she...swallowed. Is *that* something you can answer?"

All humor leaves Charon's face as suddenly as he smoked into the club. "It is possible. Especially if she has any demon venom in her as well."

"I'm sure I got all the traces of venom, but I am not as clear on the demon spunk. It isn't something I've encountered before," I admit.

The demon's eyes widen just a fraction. "How did you get the venom out?"

Just as I am about to answer, Charon's face hardens, his eyes glowing fiercely.

"I-I used To—"

"I have to go." Without any explanation, Charon is gone, leaving a fog of smoke behind.

Turning to Feather, whose eyes are as wide as I imagine mine to be, I am flabbergasted. "What the hell was that?!" I demand.

Chapter Eight

Styx

*G*OOD THING HE ANSWERED *all your questions before he took off.*

"Now what?" I ask Feather, ignoring my inner voice for once.

"We can try getting her tested," she suggests.

I can't hide the scoff that escapes my lips. "I can see it now...Yes, Doc, we need a pregnancy test for demon spawn. You have those, right? Oh, and don't worry if the baby has horns or a spiky tail." Laughing until tears sting my eyes, I shake my head.

"Whether the child is demon or not...a pregnancy test will show us if there is even anything to worry about. I'll have all the girls tested tomorrow, go from there." Feather leaves almost as quickly as Charon did, instead of smoke, her high heels click away at the wooden floor.

Over the years, I've learned not to argue with Feather, especially not when she is walking away from a conversation. She is the type to speak her mind and to hell with anyone who disagrees. That she kept her peace while Charon was here is absolutely amazing. She must either have crazy respect or crazy fear of the demon.

"Whatevs...I guess we will deal with Nova and whatever may or may not be growing in her belly another time. Good talk," I say to the empty space of the bar.

What are you going to do now?

"I am going to drink a few of these drinks Charon left behind. Then I am going to find something long and stiff to stuff myself with to the point that this day is nothing but a distant bad memory." Picking up one of the dozen shot glasses, I toss it back without flinching at the burn going down my throat. I relish in it, actually.

You do realize that it is going to take a lot more than a few drinks to even begin to numb yourself, right? What a petulant asshole that other side of me is.

"I'm aware, dick gobbler. But it sure is fun trying." I slam the last of the shot glasses down. "Now for that fuck pole." I slip off the stool and walk towards the door. Walking out of the darkness of the club, I'm surprised by the bright morning sunlight. I hadn't realized I'd been talking to Charon long enough for the night to completely pass us by.

Not going to find a quick fuck this time of day. My other self actually sounds pleased about this.

"What the hell is with the chipper tone, asshole?"

Your head is spinning. You need sleep, the voice says, brushing me off. I want to argue, but instead, I let loose a loud, drawn-out yawn.

"Okay. Fuck. You win this time." With my plans changed, I go inside to get my stuff from my locker before making the quick trip home. I go through my normal routine; lock the door, put my crucifix on its stand, and Tod on his rack. My clothes are stripped off and just tossed onto the floor as I walk to the bathroom.

While I wait for the water to heat in the shower, I scrub my face free from my "stage" makeup. I brush out my hair, tossing the bobby pins on the side of the small sink. My face is red from exfoliating as I climb in the old, clawfoot tub. The water pressure sucks, but the heat is phenomenal. It stings the sensitive skin on my face, and I groan with pleasure. The sound echoing in the small space. I know it won't take long for the heat to lose its nearly burning temp, so I begrudgingly finish my shower before drying off and curling up in bed.

"Please let me sleep the day away," is my last thought as I close my eyes.

Chapter Nine

Unknown

*Y*ou've *had a rough few days, Styx, and I'm sorry. I wish I can tell you that it will all be better soon, but I can't make that promise to you. By the Gods, I wish I knew what the future holds for you, or even what story makes up your past.*

I do not possess the power to read into your stored memories like Charon can. He may be the only one who could really fill in those blanks for you. I don't trust him, but I am quite biased. Whatever you do, please, don't let your guard down with him. He is just another demon. Famous and feared, but a demon, nonetheless.

Watching over Styx as she sleeps soundly for the first time in days, guilt washes over me. Being able to see her is a new thing that I can't get enough of. Nor can I figure out how it's possible. For heaven only knows how long, I've been in a dark, metallic prison. Unable to see my hand in front of my face...and that just barely. Over the last month, the walls have become more and more transparent. At first it was having light to banish away the never-ending darkness. Now I can see shadows beyond the walls, people moving about and all that.

I can't see details, yet—if ever—but I can tell Styx from the other shadow people. Maybe it is her energy, her aura. The familiarity of her. After decades of being at her side, it stands to reason that there would be a sort of...bond between us. Of course, she believes I am a split personality that has manifested because of what she is.

That's where a lot of my guilt comes from. I can't tell her the truth. Not yet.

Styx's whimpering pulls me out of my own thoughts. Her shadow body is thrashing around on her bed. Another nightmare. You'd think demons wouldn't be capable of having them. Creating them, yes. Having them? Not so much. But she has them. And often. I've found that singing to her helps banish whatever plagues her subconscious mind.

Ancient words pour along our mental connection. A sweet tune my mother sang to me when the darkness tried to pull me under. A lullaby of light, peace, and freedom to banish the evil and conquer the darkness.

I have to sing it a second time before Styx's body settles back against the mattress. The whimpers are replaced with soft snoring. I imagine a small smile playing at her lips as I finish the final verse.

Her lips. Are they plump or thin? I can't help but wonder what details make up her face. About the only thing I know for certain is that her eyes are red. Not only because she is a demon, but because she has special contacts to help cover the color when needed.

Thoughts of what Styx looks like follow me into my dreams as I finally let sleep take me.

Chapter Ten

Styx

A S I GET READY for another night at the French Tickler, I find myself humming. It isn't a song I can place. Hell, I can't even think if there are lyrics to it, just a melody that is soft and soothing. It is going to drive me batshit crazy trying to figure out where I've heard it. I make a mental note to ask Sam, the DJ at the club.

After a quick and sadly cold shower, I pull open my small closet door. My 'day clothes' are mostly black, off black, true black, and darkest black. Pushing those aside, I flip through my more colorful work clothes. Dark purples, dark blues...none of those strike my fancy, though, so I move on to the 80s themed neons. "Righteous! Let's go retro tonight!"

Pulling a neon green mini dress with more holes than material from a cushioned hanger, I decide on a hot pink thong and bra set. The dress has never been worn, having bought it shortly after starting at the Tickler. I had it in my head that bright was the way to go. Always. But once I actually started, I realized I could have my own theme and style. Feather isn't a pimp; she doesn't control every aspect of our jobs.

Are you going to actually put the stuff on or are you going to gawk at it until you're late?

"You are such a Nervous Nelly. I have plenty of time." I brush off my other half and stall a moment more before going to my *delicates* dresser. Panties in one drawer, bras in the other two. Every bra has a matching pair of thongs and boy shorts, but when your tits are hefty, the bras take up a lot more room. I snag the hot pink thong and bra.

Within minutes, I am dressed and pulling a pair of neon green, lace-up platform shoes from the shelf in the closet. Again. Another purchase from the early days. I slip those into my velvet drawstring bag, so they don't get scuffed on my speed run to the club. I toss in a couple pairs of thigh high stockings and a garter to put on later before cinching the bag closed.

Deciding to save my hair and makeup for the club, I toss my supplies into—what we in the biz call—a Stripper Bag. It has everything I need for a night at work; wipes, tampons, makeup, dry shampoo, and other hair products, toothbrush and paste, Grip Aid for the pole, and lots and lots of water. The main difference between mine and most of the gals I work with is the self-made hidden pocket for holy water.

Packed up and ready for work, I slip the heavy chain of my crucifix around my neck—tripling the chain around my neck so it acts as a choker—and strap Tod to my thigh, grab my bags, and zip out the door of my apartment. My demon speed, and my uncanny ability to control shadows, has me at the French Tickler—a normally fifteen-minute walk—in less than five.

I walk in through the back entrance of the club with more than enough time to do my 80s hair and makeup. I'm talking full-on width and height on this head of mine. I really should talk the girls into theme nights.

"Styx, you are rockin' that Aqua Net, babe!" Skyla bumps her hip into my thigh as she pulls curling rods from her own magenta locks.

"I don't think they even make Aqua Net anymore," I tease, adding more hairspray to my already stiff-as-fuck bangs.

"Welp, you have that 80s vibe down. Now I'm bummed. We should all do a decade theme sometime." Skyla sprays her hair to hold the beach waves in place.

Shortly after, I crawl across the stage as Def Leppard's Joe Elliott says, "Love me like a bomb," and the electric guitar begins to tear through the speakers. The blacklights make my neon clothes glow as the men begin to hoot at my movements. Just as the drums come in, the blacklights give way to regular club lights. And the men go wild.

Positioned so that the pole is behind me, I pull up into a squat, so the warm metal is aligned with my spine. I spread my knees apart, then, as I rise, I slowly close my legs. My body moves in time with the music. Hips swaying, the neon green dress moving against my skin, rising up my thighs.

Reaching out my arm, I grip the pole with my right hand, stepping halfway around it before hooking my right knee around the metal. Kicking off with my left foot, I spin around the pole. Landing on the same beat as the drum, my platforms stomping on the floor, I pull the mini dress over my head.

My neon bra and thong cause the men to hoot louder. As the song beats on, I climb the pole, wrap my legs around it and lean backward, hands stretched above my head. Now that I am upside down, I slip my bra off, letting my large breasts free.

From the odd position, all the men look like they are jeering instead of sporting lustful, greedy smiles. Their eyes are glassy, pupils wide, as they take in every inch of my tits and taut stomach. I run my hands upwards to where the strings of my neon pink thong are resting on my hips. Hooking my thumbs into the thin straps, I pull and tug on them, teasing the patrons that much more.

After the wanted response, I slip my hands between my thighs and latch onto the pole, bringing my head back above my feet. Humping the pole jiggles my ass and pushes the thoughts of sex into their horny minds even more.

Pour Some Sugar on Me is winding down, and I do some splits as I spin. Then, slide seductively down the pole, slamming my feet to the ground. I finish the song out on my knees, sliding the thong from my hips, before dropping down into a version of downward dog. From this angle, my very core is exposed to the men, and they are all but choking the chicken in their seats! I slide my knees apart, thrusting my hips towards the floor in time with the last thumps of the song.

I collect my money, jiggling for the men as they press money into my hands. Some trail thin stacks of bills down one of my tits, flicking the nipple before I snatch the money from them. Eddie is sitting off to the side, watching me with hungry eyes and a glistening of drool at the corner of his mouth. For the first time ever, I catch some creeper vibes off the regular.

Chapter Eleven

Styx

W ITH MY MONEY SECURED with my holy water, I pull my street clothes from my bag. Taking my stripper shoes off, I slip on a black thong and matching bra. My leather pants slide over my thighs and hips smoothly, hugging my curves. The secret to wearing leather pants is to beat the shit out of them until they are soft. Still strong enough to protect my skin, the material is more like a newborn kitten's fur. As I pull a black tank top over my hard as fuck hair, a dull tingle tickles at the base of my skull. A different sensation than when a demon is breaking a law, and one I haven't felt before.

Instantly on edge, I pull Tod from his sheath that was nestled inside my bag. I whirl around in a blur, dropping into a defensive pose.

Standing in the doorway is Eddie. In all the time I've been here, none of the patrons have ever come back to the dressing room. My initial shock at seeing one of my regulars in the inner sanctum washes away quickly as one twisted scenario after another races through my mind.

Without breaking my stance or eye contact, I plaster a fake smile on my face. "What are you doing back here, Eddie? Feather'll have your ass if she catches you."

"I needed to..." Eddie runs his fingers through his gray hair. His eyes go wide for the briefest of moments before zeroing in on my chest. Being a stripper—and having enormous cans—I'm used to being ogled, but something about this isn't sitting right.

Eddie takes slow steps towards me. I stand my ground.

"You really should turn around and leave, Eddie. This space isn't for customers," I remind him. I hope his lowered inhibitions are alcohol induced. No matter the cause, I can handle him. But I'd hate to put a serious hurt on him if he's just chemically fucked up.

"I won't be doing that," he sneers. His voice is different too. His speech isn't slurred, and I don't smell more than a bottle of beer on his breath.

"That isn't a healthy answer, Eddie. Would you like to rethink that?" Anyone else...anyone at all...wouldn't have this chance. Not with me. But this is Eddie. Sweet-natured, retired Eddie. The human who boasts about his grandkids to anyone who will listen. Maybe he is having one of those aneurysms humans have sometimes, making him act out of character.

I ease my stance slightly, still ready to defend myself and subdue Eddie.

"Don't scream," he whispers. His voice has more fear laced into it than one would expect from an attacker.

"The only screaming I do is in the bedroom. What the hell is all this about, Eddie?" I figure if I keep saying his name, he will snap out of whatever bullshit this is.

"Never mind. I-I just." Eddie shakes his head, his eyes clearing before they snap wide open. "Styx?!" With that, he turns and stumbles out of the door, back into the main part of the club.

What. The. Fuck?

That was—

"Fucking weird," I finish my other self's thought out loud. I've never seen him like that before. Not that the guys that come in here are all perfectly groomed and just here for the coffee, but...Eddie is one of the good ones that just enjoys the show. He tips well, drinks a few beers, and chats with the girls like they are his best friends. Probably the only friends he has aside from Kenny.

Shaking my head, I sheathe Tod and stalk out of the dressing room to find Feather. She may have to put a restriction on Eddie for a little bit. For the girls' safety, and his own. If he puts one finger out of place...

I scan the club for Eddie and spot Feather behind the bar. Not that I expect him to still be here, but just on the off chance he is dumb enough to have stuck around. Stepping behind the bar, I lean on the counter next to my boss.

"What's up, Styx?" Feather asks as she wipes water spots from a beer mug.

"Have you talked to Eddie tonight?"

"Just to give him a beer. Why?"

Filling Feather in on everything from the moment I made eye contact with him from the stage to him stumbling out of the backroom, I watch as her jaw clenches and her eyes search the club. Feather has a lot of rules to keep her girls safe, and the regulars like Eddie and Kenny know them by heart. Hell, there have been times that I've heard one or both of them explaining them to the newbies. Words of Wisdom from the old geezers, they called i t.

"No tingles?" Feather asks when I finished.

"Just that someone was behind me. No demonic tingle," uttering the last bit quieter.

"I'll put him on a time-out." Which translates to him being banned for a week or two. "Might bring it up to Charon, too. Make sure nothing got to the graybeard."

I look at her with probably the same surprised look Eddie gave me. I hadn't thought that he could have been under some kind of demonic influence.

Fuck me sideways and call me Earl.

Chapter Twelve

Styx

A SSURED THAT FEATHER IS going to handle the Eddie sitch, I gather my things and go home. The whole thing sticks in my mind like a thorn in my paw. I just can't shake the way his eyes looked when he told me not to scream. I hadn't realized it then, but they didn't have that twinkle in them that he usually has when chatting with me. Or maybe I am just imagining things and he was just drunker than normal.

As I close my door, I throw the lock in place as an afterthought. I can handle just about anything that is dumb enough to walk into my place, but I'm not going to make it easy. Before walking away from the door, I slide the dead bolt too. It hasn't been used in all the time I've lived here so it sticks a little. Nothing my demon strength can't handle, though. With a little effort, the rusty post thunks into place.

Moving deeper into the apartment, I toss my bag on the bed and unload everything. This is the boring part, making sure things are put back into their place and restocked for the next night. I should leave it for tomorrow, but who the fuck knows what will happen between now and then. Damn demons always screw my plans.

Running straight hot water in the kitchen sink, I mix some Borax in, watching it dissolve as I swish it around with my hand. As I slip each bill in, I'm surprised to see more tens and twenties than singles. Guess it pays to switch things up a bit.

I roll my shoulders as I make my way to the bathroom. Dreading, but also excited, to wash all this shit out of my hair. The knots have knots and are all glued together with hairspray. It's going to take some work to look like myself, but that sink full of dough makes the hassle worth it.

Turning on the hot water, and only the hot water, I strip off my clothes and step under the stream. The near lava-like water penetrates my hair, runs in tiny rivers over my scalp. In some way, that is more relaxing than a massage. And, if I'm being honest, a bit orgasmic.

As the water cascades over my skin, turning it a brilliant shade of red, I find myself humming that song again. The cadence is calming, almost hypnotic.

I hum as I dump the second round of conditioner into my hair, working all the tangles out with a comb. The scent of coconut masks every other scent this bathroom usually has—thanks to the old tenants who smoked like it was going out of style—as it smooths my hair to its normal, straight self.

And then my nose is assaulted by the pungent odor of sulfur.

Fuck!

With conditioner dripping from my hair to the tiled floor, I snag Tod from the back of the toilet and bolt out of the bathroom. Sword held out in front of me, ready for any attack, I freeze when I see the remnants of red smoke curling around Charon.

"What the hell, Charon?! Doors exist!" Stomping over to my dresser, I pull out a t-shirt left behind by a one-nighter. Normally I toss them, but this one has Elvira on it.

"Yes, yes. Knock-knock. I'm here now." Charon brushes me off as he tosses a towel to me, which I wrap around my hair.

"You aren't going to just pop in whenever you want now, are you?"

"Styx, will you drop the human normalities for five minutes? You need to come with me." Charon takes a step closer.

"Explain?" Hoping the ancient being will at least extend that courtesy to me, I pull on the pair of shorts that were lying on the floor.

"You need education, and I want to test a theory." His words are rushed, and a bit exasperated as if he's had to repeat himself to a two-year-old.

"Can I at least rinse my hair first?"

Charon snaps his fingers, and the towel falls to the floor, my hair—now dry as a bone and conditioner free—drops down my back.

Cool!

"Uh...thanks. Where are we going?" I ask, strapping Tod's sheath to my back. The demon even dressed me in my comfy travel clothes. Ie: leather pants and black tank stretching across my boobs.

"Darlin', we are goin' to Hell."

Chapter Thirteen

Kyon

A RIPPLE RUNS DOWN my spine as someone enters Hades' domain. Sticking my nose in the thick, hot air, I pull in a breath. The beings who enter hell all have distinctive scents. Souls carry the pungent stank of fear—most of them, anyway. A rare few smell remorseless, uncaring of what their fate will be.

That isn't what I smell, though. What greets me is the mixture of sulfur, cinnamon, and nature. Charon has returned from Topside again. Only this time, there is something more. Something beyond what Charon calls flowers, grass, and mortals; the scents of Topside. No, this is the most intriguing thing I've ever scented. Even more so than when Charon brought down something called frankincense. I don't know what to categorize the aroma as, but I know deep within my soul that I need to know what it is.

I make my way over to where Charon's boat docks and wait for him. He has brought something different from Topside again. My belly flutters with anticipation as the faint light from the lantern that hangs on the bow of Charon's skiff comes into view. The hellfire within the lantern lights the way for Charon as he ferries souls down the Rivers Styx and Acheron.

Through the mists, I can see the silhouette of the boat and two figures on board. One of them is obviously Charon, but the creature he has with him is not a soul. I can't make out any features, but I see long hair flowing behind the unknown. And my heart flutters to life.

Chapter Fourteen

Styx

A CRISP SNAP ECHOES in my ears as Charon smokes us to the outskirts of the Underworld. A little pissed that he didn't give me any warning, I ask why he doesn't just poof us to where we are going.

"Well, my dear, what fun would that be? You'd miss the whole experience of traveling the glorious river you are named for," he replies in a way that I am finding quite pompous.

Okay, maybe I am less pissed now. I have always wanted to ride the river the way the souls do. Does that make me morbid? Maybe. But it also makes me hardcore as fuck.

Charon doesn't say a word as we walk. He doesn't hum, snap his fingers, or even breathe loudly. So, I look around casually, trying not to look as excited as I am. Sure, I've been to the Underworld a time or two, but never like this.

The only part of the Underworld I have ever seen were the enormous caverns where Malkiss lives and works. Malkiss, aka Kinvallatas, one of the top demons of torture in the Underworld, aka the closest thing I've ever had to a father.

I didn't grow up in the Underworld, but once my demon powers began to...manifest, I somehow ended up in Malkiss' parlor. I must have been about seven at the time. Scared shitless and utterly confused, I stood in front of the demon with the bulbous head and terrifying horns.

He could have killed me. As I became older, visiting as often as I could, he probably wished he had. I have not always been the sweet bitch I am now.

To see more of the Underworld is something I've always wanted to do, but Malkiss forbade it. So, to say I am excited to explore this strange and new area of the Underworld is the understatement of the year. However, I refuse to let Charon know that.

"Just around this bend," Charon states, leaving me to wonder what is around the bend.

"Are you doing that cryptic shit the old timers are known for?"

"Nope."

Devil damnit, he is annoying as fuck! Why does he not tell me anything about where we are? All I get is 'just around this bend.' How hard would it be to say we are in the northwest corner of Hell where such and such a place exists?

I'm about to open my bitch mouth when a soft, green glow breaks through the darkness. With each step, the light becomes stronger until a glowing river comes into view.

"It's beautiful," I breathe out.

Stretching as far as the eye can see, the River Styx flows with the ethereal green glow from the torbernite that borders its shores. To the souls who are brought across on Charon's boat, the image is meant to be harrowing. To me, though, it is the most serene place I've ever been to.

"Isn't it? Styx, meet Styx," Charon chuckles at his pathetic attempt at a joke.

Glaring at the ancient demon, I shake my head. "Is that the best you got, really?" He only shrugs.

Then I see it. Almost as beautiful as the river herself, Charon's skiff floats motionless on the moving water. The whole thing appears to be made from skulls and bones. Each piece as ageless as the Underworld itself.

At the bow is the largest skull of them all. It resembles a vulture, complete with a beak, but is much, much larger. Set where its eyes once were are glowing embers of brimstone, I'd be willing to bet. From the beak hangs a lantern made of what appears to be brushed bronze, but I'm not certain. What makes it stunning are the crystals projecting the eternal flames far and wide.

"What do you think?" Charon asks as he sweeps an arm towards his skiff.

"It's breathtaking!" Carefully stepping over the torbernite, I get closer to the bony boat. I reach a hand to run my fingers over the closest skull. A zing races up from the tip of my fingers all the way up my arm. Jerking back, I angrily growl out, "What the fuck was that?!"

"What do you mean, darlin'?" The confusion is evident in Charon's voice as he steps closer. His eyebrows are drawn down, and he is looking at me like I've gone mad.

"Your fucking boat zapped me like a damn live wire!" I rub my numb arm as I glare at the old piece of shit boat. And to think I was falling in love with the damned thing!

"It can't be." He sounds awestruck.

"I'm sure your boat has never shocked your ancient ass, but it sure as fuck shocked me! Why the fuck would it do that?"

"I have my theories. And it seems they are playing out exactly as I thought they would." Charon steps into his asshole of a boat and reaches a hand out to me.

"You're joking. I am *not* stepping foot on that...that...literal death machine!"

Charon howls with laughter, the sound echoing through the caverns, sounding awesomely creepy. Once his laughter settles to random chuckles, he says, "She won't bite you again. I promise."

Tentatively, I put my hand in his and step over the edge of Sparky's side. Yup. I am totally calling this bitch Sparky.

As the sole of my boot touches the floor of the boat, I wait, hoping the rubber will prevent any further shocks. Satisfied, I climb in, careful to not touch anything.

"I don't have any obol to pay you. Can I owe you?" I snicker.

Charon rolls his eyes as he uses a long staff to push us from the shore. Almost immediately, the water begins to swell and move, yet the skiff doesn't rock or sway in the slightest.

"Relax, Styx. You won't get shocked again. I know you are *dying* to explore her."

"Your jokes are as old as you are, old man." My curiosity is getting the better of me as I reach for a femur poking up like a handle. When the tip of my first finger makes contact, I jerk back before timidly going back. It doesn't shock me this time.

I excitedly run both hands around the bones and skulls, inside as giddy as a schoolgirl. "Did you build this skiff?" I inquire, feeling more relaxed now that Sparky isn't trying to kill me.

"No. I can't take the credit for that. However, I did acquire the majority of the bones for it. Hunting and defeating the Rukh for the bow was the hardest part."

"Worth it, though." Marveling over how smoothly the skiff moves through the water, souls and all, I lean over the edge. I peer into the green and white glowing water in an attempt to figure out how the boat moves. Obviously, there's no motor, no oars either. Damn, I love magic!

A thin veil of mist stretches in front of us as if it tries to block our path. Charon doesn't flinch as Sparky floats right through it. For a few seconds, the mist separates me from Charon. The cool fingers of the mist are such a contrast to the heat of Hell that goosebumps coat my skin.

Then just as suddenly as we pierce that veil, we are leaving it behind.

"See over there?" Charon points to a dock that juts out over the river. "That is where we are going to start our adventure."

We haven't started yet? I suppose riding up and down the rivers isn't very exciting to him anymore after millions of years.

There is something just beyond the dock, but I can't quite make it out. "What is that?" I ask.

Before Charon answers me, the silhouette becomes more detailed. As we float closer, the creature becomes more and more visible.

Standing on four tree trunk-sized legs is the most massive being I've ever seen. A long serpentine tail slithers back and forth in the air. Ridges of some sort line its back.

The creature turns around and I gape in awe. No, surprise. Nope. Fear. Yeah, let's go with all of that. Three...yes, I counted right...three huge dog heads and six glowing eyes are all glaring right at me.

Chapter Fifteen

Kyon

AS THE SKIFF DRAWS closer, cutting through the mist, I'm absolutely mesmerized by the beauty that stands behind Charon. Long brown hair dips over her shoulders and hangs down her back. Like diamonds, the mist clings to strands of her hair for a brief moment.

Her eyes, as blood red as Charon's, hold the sparkle of curiosity and awe as they try to look everywhere at once. The moment her gaze lands on me, I feel it.

Sniffing with my noses in the air.

I sense a barrage of emotions flitting over her just as easily as I see them play across her features. My heart plummets when one of those emotions is fear.

That is new for me. Of course, this whole experience is new to me, but being distraught because I cause fear? That is one of the reasons I am one of the many guardians of the Underworld.

This female, though, I don't want to scare her. I want to curl up at her feet and guard her for the rest of my life.

That's what I must do! I think to myself, I need to look less imposing. So as not to startle her any further, I slowly drop down to my belly. I force my snake tail to settle, to wrap around me to appear less threatening. Putting all sets of my ears down, I lay my chins on my paws.

"He won't bite. See? He is lying down like a good puppy!"

"Puppy? That is *not* a puppy. Puppies fit into the crook of your arm, or even on your lap. *That* is a freaking Cerberus!"

Sorrowful whines in three different pitches escape my lips.

"You've hurt his feelings, Styx. That is just poor etiquette." Charon shakes his head. "Come. Off the boat." He holds his hand towards her.

"If that thing tries to eat me, I will introduce it to Tod," she threatens.

"Styx, you are not a damned soul, nor are you a law-breaking demon. You have nothing to fear from him. Let me introduce you."

She seems to consider what she's been told before taking Charon's hand and allowing him to lead her to me. Once on solid ground, she reaches behind her back and pulls a toothpick, sorry, I mean sword, from under her hair.

"If he so much as growls at me, I'm going to run him through."

I chuff. That tiny thing couldn't damage me if a thousand demons wielded it at once.

"Find that funny, fleabag?"

"Styx. Meet Kyon. He is the highest-ranking Cerberus Hell has to offer. Kyon, this is Styx, grade A pain in the ass."

Chapter Sixteen

Styx

"**G** Grade A pain in the ass? Okay, I'll give you that." Hey, I may not know much about demons and Hell, but I sure as fuck know I am a pain in the ass. And a bitch. But that's neither here nor there. "What does it mean to be a high ranking Cerberi?"

"Usually, it means they are the best at their job. For Kyon, though, it's more than that. He is the second born of Typhon and Echidna and first of the Cerberi," Charon explains.

"So...he's the original. King of the Cerberi...so to speak," I offer.

The large, three-headed dog chuffs, his breath causing a dust storm to swirl around us.

Coughing, I pull my tight tank top shirt up and duck my face behind it. Fucking mongrel! My guess is he doesn't have the common sense in *any* of his heads to turn the other way. Keep the souls where they belong, fuck manners, the end.

A sharp snap surprises me before Charon says, "You can stop ogling your breasts, Styx. The storm is gone."

Popping up from my shirt, I glare at him. "Not my fault the three-headed mongrel doesn't have enough sense to do that shit in a different direction!"

Vibrations begin to tickle my feet before increasing in intensity, enough so that I am nearly knocked on my ass! The quake is accompanied by a rumbling growl which is magnified by the three different mouths it escapes from.

I dig my fingers into my ears, but it doesn't stop the noise. "ALL RIGHT! COOL IT! I'M SORRY, OKAY?" I scream, and the noise stops immediately.

"Kyon, my apologies for her poor manners. She has been around humans too long." I barely hear Charon's voice over the ringing in my ears.

The giant dog nods his middle head, the other two are busy looking at me. The concept is freaky and unnerving.

Don't get me wrong, I love the freaky stuff. Except for demons who think they can do whatever they want to whomever they want to do it to, of course. I'd rather curl up with a good horror movie...cheesy or downright chilling...than watch chick flicks. The Spirit Halloween store is my home away from Hell, but having two sets of eyes blooming with the fires of Hell boring into my soul?

Shaking myself mentally, I focus instead on the middle set of eyes. The ones that are looking at Charon while pretending—and failing—to ignore the other two. Maybe if I look beyond the heads, I can settle my nerves.

This frazzled feeling pisses me off. I don't get frazzled. Okay, that once with Eddie at the club...but that wasn't really him. I'm a stone-cold bitch who kills demons and saves lives. Demons. My freaking brethren! Demons who have horns and acidic saliva have perished at my blade. A few angry puppy eyes staring down at me should be a walk in the park!

Fine, the 'puppy' in question is like thirty feet tall, at least. His teeth are about as long as I am tall, and instead of a wagging tail, he has a fucking anaconda! Seriously. The thing weaves and bobs in the air, its tongue flicking about, scenting the air.

As if the serpent senses my attention, its large head turns towards me. Beady eyes peer at me as the head tilts to the side. A few flicks of its tongue and it creeps closer to me.

Fuck. Fuck. Fuckity fuck!

It isn't venomous. Oh! NOW my inner voice wants to talk!

Maybe not, but I still don't want its attention on me. Fucker can squeeze the life out of me. It may not be the best, but I have grown quite attached to living, I retort.

Inching closer still, the serpent stops about an arm's length away. I could easily slice its head off with Tod from this distance. But the sword remains at my side.

Sensual.

Fierce.

Protective.

Each word drifts into my head like my other personality's voice does. But not exactly. This voice is raspy and slow, as if it's choosing its words with the utmost care. For some reason, I get the feeling that the serpent is talking to me.

"Was that you?" I ask while pointing at the anaconda tail.

It pulls its head back slightly and then...I swear to Satan...nods!

"Why those words? How are you talking in my head? What the fuck are you?" I blurt out in one breath.

That is what I scent from you, it replies cautiously. ***I am as surprised as you are that you can hear me.*** The serpent looks down its thick body, seemingly following along to where it ends, and the Cerberus' body starts.

I expect a smart-ass remark like 'a tail' to filter into my mind. Instead, the snake says, ***I am part of Kyon.*** I can hear the shrug in its words as if the obvious is the norm and goes without explanation.

"Who are you talking to?" Charon interrupts.

"Apparently the tail. That thing literally has a mind all its own." I point to the being in question.

"Fascinating," he whispers.

"No more cryptic shit. You brought me here for a reason, and I highly doubt it has anything to do with Kyon." I'm getting testy. The eons old demon has yet to tell me why he dragged me to Hell, and my curiosity is wearing my patience down to the nub.

Husky laughter answers my demands. "We are here to test a theory, one that is going to tell me who you are."

"Dementia much? I'm Styx. Stripper and demon hunter extraordinaire. There isn't much more to know." I gave up trying to fill in the blanks of my past. Whatever it is, it's probably best left unknown. My parents obviously didn't want me, Hell never came to claim me, and I've become accustomed to who I am. I don't need some deep-rooted family tree to define me. It wouldn't change a damn thing, anyway.

As if reading my mind, he asks, "Don't you want to know what the visions you saw mean?" He has me there. While I honestly don't care about the neglectful parents I had, I sure as hellfire want to know what that vision was.

"Be patient for just a little longer, Styx. Please?"

I was prepared to tell him to shove it up his ass until he said please. He seems almost desperate to answer my life's questions. Why does he even care?

"On one condition. You need to tell me why you are so vested in this." Staring at him, I wait for him to answer or tell me to forget the whole thing.

"If you are who I believe you to be, then our fates are more intertwined than just our common friend."

"That is still pretty cryptic, old devil. Care to elaborate?" I hike my hand up, rotating my wrist, gesturing for him to give me more information.

"If I tell you my theory, and I am wrong, there could be dire consequences. For both of us."

Chapter Seventeen

Styx

AFTER THAT OMINOUS STATEMENT, Charon walks off, waving a hand for me to follow. Still not knowing what the fuck is going on, or even where he is planning on taking me, I follow along with my arms crossed over my chest. I want to be excited about what this trip could possibly mean for me, but I am not the type that likes surprises. Especially ones that require the words 'dire consequences.'

I look over my shoulder as we walk away, half expecting the giant Cerberus to be following. He is still where we left him, all three heads are tilted in different directions, all eyes on me. Even the serpent tail seems to be watching me.

"So, you aren't going to give me a hint?"

Charon glances at me but doesn't say anything at first. "I believe I know from whom you came. We are going to find that out now."

I stumble to a stop as if the soles of my shoes melted to the heated rocks. "My parents? You are taking me to meet my parents?!" My words are a strained shriek. Suddenly, I'm unable to breathe around the lump in my throat.

"Quiet down, little one," Charon looks around quickly. "I'm confident that I am at least close in my theory, but we must be sure before we go celebrating with a reunion."

Scratching at my collarbone, I take a step closer to the ancient. What if my parents abandoned me because they didn't want me? They're demons, they might not have an ounce of love in them for me. What if they kill me on sight?

On that note, what if they take it out on Charon for trying to reconnect them with the offspring they dumped Topside? This is a bad idea. A very, *very* bad idea.

"I think we should snuff this plan of yours," I blurt out, causing him to whirl around and stare at me.

Intense moments stretch on for what feels like hours as Charon seems to attempt to make sense of me...or the meaning of life. Who the hell knows?

"Why?" Just one simple word with so much hiding behind it. He doesn't seem disappointed or angry, only curious as he cocks one eyebrow up.

Biting my lip, I try to come up with a less paranoid-damsel-in-distress answer that he will find acceptable. I don't want to show my weakness to him. Especially not in the bowels of Hell...who knows who could be listening.

At least that's what I'm telling myself my concern is.

You are afraid. Admit it to him. Damn that inner me.

"You said dire consequences. While I can handle anything that comes my way..."

Lies.

"If it has you worried for your own safety, I don't want to risk that. I mean...what could possibly scare a demon of your experience and stature?"

Yeah, make it about him. He is only millions of years old, he won't see right through that, my other personality snaps sarcastically.

I ignore myself.

Charon smiles knowingly. "It certainly isn't *my* safety I am worried about. Upsetting the wrong gods or goddesses can result in the rivers running dry."

At my confused features, Charon continues with a sigh as if he's made this speech before. Or maybe it's because I should automatically understand what that would mean. "If the rivers go dry, what do you think would become of the trapped souls? The oaths made on the shores of the River Styx?"

I take a minute to think it over. The only answers that I can grasp are the most obvious. "The souls would be free, and the oaths would be null and void. Seems like a win-win." I shrug.

"Free. Yes, the souls would be *free* to wreak havoc. They would rally and wage war against the gods, goddesses, and demons who've kept them in their prison." The fire in Charon's eyes flares to life as the picture he paints plays in my mind.

Realizing what those repercussions truly mean, I shiver. "And the oaths?" I ask, curiosity getting the better of me.

"Let's just say...you don't want that to happen." The threat and warning in his voice are enough to make me press my lips together.

"With all due respect, Charon, my lineage is not so important as to risk those types of ramifications. I may be a hard bitch, but I don't want to be the cause for that kind of upset. I have survived this long not knowing who gave me life and I will continue to strive...one way or another." Adulting, am I right?

As I wait for him to say something, Charon stares at me contemplatively. He does that a lot, and it's beginning to drive me a little batty.

"If you truly feel that way, I will bring you back to Topside," he states.

Without giving it another thought, I nod. Surprised when his shoulders droop by the most miniscule degree. Whether the action is because of his relief at avoiding war, or disappointment, I have no clue.

Charon snaps his fingers. When the smoke clears, I find myself standing in the center of my small apartment. Alone.

Chapter Eighteen

Styx

"R Rude," I announce to the empty room. I would probably feel silly for it if it wasn't something I did often...talking to myself out loud. Sometimes I responded, but usually by way of the pesky split personality.

Grabbing my half-packed bag, I go through my closet and toss some options in before concealing them behind the zipper. It will take me mere seconds to get to the club, but I hate having to rush. Tonight, I feel like soaking in the atmosphere on my way.

Comparing the Underworld to the lush greens of my world, I honestly can't decide which I like best. Of course, the doom and gloom, the fire pits, and the unknown of the Underworld are enticing. All of it sings to a part of me—my demon side, of course—as if begging me to return to it. To live among the other demons, to relish in the heat, and to dance with the damned.

On the other hand, there is much that I enjoy about living Topside, as the demons call it. The changing seasons, hoodies in the fall and winter, and the people! Oh, the people! Most of them, damn near all of them, piss me right the fuck off. Always looking for someone or something to blame for whatever sadness they feel in their lives or bitching and complaining because their bus was late, or someone didn't smile back.

Those are the people who are quick to feel uneasy or defensive when others smile first. As if they are suddenly in danger from a serial rapist/killer. Humans tend to jump to judge, that's for sure. In a small way, it makes me appreciate demons. They only care what their superiors think, although that is more fear-induced behavior than anything else.

Back to people, though, some of them are quite entertaining. Some of them are kind and determined to live life to its fullest. Feather is a prime example of that. She had a rough life, from what I understand. From bad relationships to being broken and living on the streets, she has seen it all, experienced it all. Now she runs one of the cleanest and best strip joints in the US and has her life just the way she wants it. I want to be Feather when I grow up.

Both places have their own appeal. I don't think I could ever choose one over the other. All I need to do is come up with a way to have the best of both worlds.

Taking the long way into work, I take in the warm streetlamps separating the street from the sidewalk. This area is nice, clean, and more upscale than where I live. The homes are all houses, not crumbling apartment buildings, with brick faces and porches. On some of these porches, there are couples enjoying the evening and a glass of wine or bottle of beer.

Jealousy rears its head as I take in the comfort and safety these humans seem to be enjoying within each other's arms. Demons don't snuggle. At least not that I have ever heard of. Demons fuck. Viciously.

Shaking my head, I cross over the tracks and dip into the darkness. Using the shadows, I move quickly and silently until I am in a puddle of black next to the dumpster behind the French Tickler. I shrug off the last remnants of my wallowing and open the door.

As I step inside, I'm nearly knocked over by an excited Frankie. Thank Nyx that we are both rich in agility and balance as we right ourselves.

"Sorry, Styx. My bad!"

"What's got you all wound up?" I ask, repositioning the strap of my bag over my shoulder.

"There are two guys out there I've never seen before. Sex on a damn stick!" Frankie makes a fist in front of her mouth, her lips making the perfect O while her tongue prods at the inside of her cheek each time her hand is close to her mouth.

"Classy, Frankie. Real classy," I tease with a roll of my eyes. I walk into our dressing room, Frankie cackles as she follows.

Chapter Nineteen

Styx

A s Panic at the Disco's *Saturday Night* begins to play, I slip across the stage and the lights turn on. Gripping the pole in my right hand, I straddle the warmed metal.

The song plays on, and I continue to grind against the pole, pretending that it's my lover. The hard metal not doing a damn thing for me, but I am making it look like it does. And these guys...they buy every minute muscle movement. Most likely imagining that I was grinding on them instead. Their horny yelps of approval sound muted compared to Brandon Urie's crooning.

After doing some twirls, handstands, and sliding down the pole with my legs wrapped around it until my hands reach the flooring of the stage. I let go of the pole and lower my feet, now standing with my barely covered ass and twat high in the air towards the crowd.

With my hands gripping my ankles, I peer between my calves at the gathered men. New faces swim in the sea of familiar ones. I sway my hips from side to side before using the pole to help me stand.

As the song comes to an end, I crawl around the edge of the stage, collecting money in my thong as I go. When I pass by Kenny and Eddie, I can't help but notice Eddie's eyes, downcast with guilt. I'll have to chat with him before he leaves for the night.

At the far end of the stage, I spot a set of nearly golden eyes watching my every move. A stalking gaze heated with intense desire, arms crossed over a broad chest, and chocolate brown hair that is both wavy and curly framing his bronze skinned face. His strong jaw ticks as he clenches his molars together.

The intensity isn't ignored as it would be if it were any other 'John' in the joint. There is something about him that makes me want to keep crawling until I am comfortably in his lap. Licking his face, marking him with my scent, and devouring his cock with my pussy.

Snap out of it, Styx! You are here to work. Nothing more. That annoying voice is right, and I lean up onto my knees, shaking my head as if I am merely trying to push my hair out of my face.

My tits shake with the movement, nipples hard from my arousal, but we will blame it on the air conditioner. Even if it isn't running. The men applaud and hoot louder.

By the time I make it to the end of the stage, sliding my knees with each step like I'm doing mini splits, the golden eyed man's jaw is nearly creaking with the ferocity. Dark brown eyebrows are arrowed down over his fire-kissed eyes. He isn't aroused. He isn't interested like the others in the club are. He looks pissed!

Maybe he's gay and got himself roped into the wrong kind of club by his straight friends.

Not to be deterred, I plant my hands on the floor in front of me, sliding my knees from under me so that I am lying flat on my belly. I roll to the right towards the crowd so that I am on my back before doing a spin kick type of move to regain my standing position.

With a flourish, I bow to my screaming and whistling fans before sashaying off the stage, leaving some bills behind me that I know Jaxton will bring up behind me. It's his job, after all, to clear the stage after each of us dance. Otherwise, we'd be scrambling around picking up bills looking both greedy and not very sexy. It disrupts the whole fantasy we've spent the entire song creating for our patrons.

Before I duck through the curtain, I take a final glance over my shoulder at Sexy McGee. His glare still on me, I shoot him a playful smile and finger wave, and I swear I hear a low growl.

"Fuck, Styx! Did you mop the floor when you were done?" Jazz asks teasingly. "I thought you were going to wrap your thighs around that guy's head!"

Battling the heat that rises to my cheeks, I turn from Jazz. In an attempt to throw her off, I ask, "What are you jabbering about?"

"The guy at the DJ's end of the stage that was watching you from the moment you stepped up to the pole. He didn't show a flinch of interest in anyone else but you. New beau?" Jazz smiles so wide I can see her wisdom teeth.

"Shit, no! I don't know who he is. Definitely never saw him around here before. Have you?" I respond. I want to know who the stranger is...something I don't normally waste a second of my life worrying about is now the only thing on my mind. Well...that and how he tastes.

Feather will skin you if you sleep with the clients.

Bite me. I can wonder all I want. Mental fucking doesn't count, I argue with my bitchier half.

"Nope. There were two of them I've never seen before. Him and his buddy. Now that one I wouldn't mind licking like a damn Tootsie pop!" Jazz mimics licking said treat.

"I wonder how many licks it takes to get to the center of that bad boy!" Skyla joins in.

"You all need to get a good dicking. All of you acting like teenage boys in the locker room," Nova complains from her chair in the corner of the dressing room. Ever since her run-in with the demon, which she thankfully doesn't remember, Nova has been a complete drag. Not that she was a barrel of monkeys before, but now she behaves like a spinster aunt who is bored with life. Hopefully, she is just in a funk, and it isn't something more serious...or worse...demon-related.

"Oh, Nova! You have NO idea! I haven't had sex in three months! This dry spell is killing me!" Frankie complains as she wipes the makeup from her face. She'd been on the floor just after me and is sitting in front of the fan.

Korra is the last act of the night, closing the show with a medley of crap music no one would ever mash together. Why she creates such garbage to dance to is beyond me.

"How long's it been for you, Styx?" Skyla asks, tossing a bottle of water to me.

"Too long," is my only answer. It's always the same answer whenever the question of sex and my personal life comes up. If I tell them it has been recent, they will pester me for details I don't want to give. Of course, too long could be a day or a year for all they know, so it isn't exactly lying.

"Maybe that guy with the bright eyes will break your dry spell." Jazz nudges my shoulder.

"No doinking the clients, girls," Nova says as plainly as if she were asking for someone to pass the milk.

"He isn't a regular, I don't think he qualifies as a client. Besides, he didn't drop a buck for any of us. Not even Styx. And he had his eyes glued to her the entire time she was out there," Jazz argues.

"He came in here. He is a client. Hands off." It's as if Nova is reciting the Gettysburg Address with as much enthusiasm as she puts into her words.

Yeah, hands off. Move along, little doggy. You should get some sleep, anyway. Never know when the next hunt will spring up.

Fuck off, I grumble mentally.

Picking up my bag, I turn towards the back door. "Peace out, girl scouts. See you on the flippy." With that, I'm back among the shadows, sucking in the cool night air. I reposition my bag, so I don't drop it as I zip back to my apartment.

Within seconds, I'm up the stairs and in the door. The light of the crescent moon barely adds a glow through the one window in this rat hole. Thank Nyx for my ability to see in the dark. I don't turn any lights on as I make my way to the kitchen to wash tonight's money. The warm glow of golden eyes turned to fire embedded in my mind.

Chapter Twenty

Kyon

W ATCHING HER SLIDE ACROSS the stage with a grace I've never witnessed before—not even from the humans who were dancing before her—ignited something inside of me that I've not ever felt in my chest in my long life. I sense the human males ogling her, their arousal at watching her body move as each strip of her clothing is removed stings my nose. They want her, crave her, but they can't have her. Not if I have anything to say about it.

Charon told me she danced for strangers to make money. He explained in vague details what that meant. I haven't ever been Topside before, so explaining these things to me, I'm sure, is a headache all within itself...judging by how many times Charon rubbed at his forehead. He left out the part where she showed off her precious parts to the roomful of sweat-soaked humans.

I cross my arms over my chest and scowl as I watch her. While my cock reacts to her, I clench my jaw. The pain of how disturbingly hard it is getting against the zipper of these human jeans on top of the fury I feel over all these men staring at her with drool seeping between their lips is causing my hound to rise to the forefront. I need to push him down, shifting to an enormous three-headed dog in the middle of the packed club would get me killed.

"That's the one, isn't it?" Ormr asks from my side.

A sharp nod is the only answer I can give him.

"She sure is beautiful, Kyon."

I nod again. I can't speak. I can't even unclench my jaw. Never in all the thousands of years I've lived have I ever had to fight this hard to hold onto my form. Ormr's remark doesn't help.

I knew from the moment I scented her that she was going to change my world and turn it upside down. Once Charon sent her back Topside, I went to Persephone and Hades and pleaded for them to allow me access to cross over. Just this once, I had promised. With bright smiles, they agreed. I honestly thought Hades would argue against letting his top Cerberus leave the Underworld, but he granted me a vacation of sorts, as long as I brought Ormr with me.

I agreed to his terms without a thought. Master has a reason for everything he does, and if you are smart, you don't question him. Persephone is the only one who dares to do so. Then again, she has Hades wrapped around her delicate fingers in all kinds of ways.

Persephone, having been Topside the most recently of the two, explained to me about human clothes and behaviors. Hades gave me one warning; "Shift Topside, even just a little, and I will have to euthanize you." It is this threat that has my jaw seconds away from dislocating.

"Hot damn," Ormr whispers breathlessly as Styx crawls across the stage, her red eyes pinned on me.

Breathe, mutt! You will die if you shift.

They want what is ours, my most possessive side growls.

These filthy beasts want to partake in carnal pleasures with our female. This from the aggressive side of me.

I won't let them touch a hair on her body. Stay back, I command them.

Their ire burns in my eyes, I can see it reflected in Styx's. Suddenly, the scent of her arousal trumps every other smell in the place. A tangy delicacy that I want to slurp up with every tongue in my possession. A flavor that I want coating my throat as I commit it to memory.

Her large breasts, which I have done my best to ignore up until now, shimmy as she tosses her hair back from her face. I want to bite them, mark them with my fangs, claim them as mine.

"Settle down, K. You can't afford to lose it now." Ormr grips my shoulder, his nails digging slightly into my skin.

Styx is suddenly up and walking away, her hips swaying perfectly with each step. She stops, looks over her shoulder, and smiles, then waggles her slim fingers at me before she disappears behind a curtain.

With her out of sight, my beast calms down substantially.

"Now what?" Ormr asks. Using his grip on my shoulder, he leads me towards the bar as the next female begins her dance.

"I don't know. I need to talk to her, but I don't know how to get to her."

"Charon didn't tell you where she lives?"

"No. Something about her bitching about privacy." I shrug, still not understanding why Charon had a grin on his face when he told me that.

"Maybe the one serving drinks will help us?" Ormr suggests.

When we reach the long table that runs along the longest wall in the building, an older female walks over to us and slaps her hands on the counter. "What will it be, boys?"

"Two drinks of the lady's choice," Ormr states. "And perhaps some information?"

"Depends on the information you want. Got I.D.?" she asks as her gaze slips over both of our faces.

"Are you Feather?" I ask.

"Depends."

"Charon sent us," I state simply, glancing down to the floorboards.

Feather's eyes light up and she places her elbows on the bar. She leans in a little closer and asks, "What are you?"

Nervously, I look over to Ormr to find he is giving me the same look. Hades didn't say we couldn't tell anyone what we are, but...

"Listen, I've kept his secret for many years. Not a soul in this place will know what you are unless you want them to." Feather leans in more. "But I have a business to run, and I need to know what kind of creatures Charon is sending my way."

Nodding, I lean in closer, my lips an inch from her ear. "We are Cerberi."

Sucking in a breath, Feather slowly leans back. "Well, ho-ly shit. I didn't know you all looked so...studly."

"Only in this form. We can be quite grotesque in our other forms," Ormr admits.

"Interesting. Welp, what can I do you for?" Feather asks, suddenly all business.

"One of your dancers has caught my friend's attention. He needs to speak with her," Ormr explains.

"Isn't that against the Accords?"

"Only if she were human." My answer seems to make something click behind her wise eyes.

"I see. I won't tell you where she lives, but she will be out back in say...five minutes as per her usual routine. But I warn ya, if she stabs you, don't come crying to me." With that, Feather walks away to help another male.

"Guess we don't get our drinks?" Ormr teases as we make our way through the crowd towards the front door.

It takes forever to reach the exit. The large male standing there opens the door for us. We walk by, nodding before we step into the night. It's freezing out here and I'm grateful to Persephone for sending us with things called jackets. She said that compared to Hell, any temperature would be extreme to us. However, she didn't want us standing out wearing thick protective gear, so she magicked some leather to be more insulated than it looks.

I lead the way to the corner of the building and turn into the dark alley. My vision adjusts so that I can see where the building corners again. That must be the back. Once we turn, I can see a few large, metal containers lining the building. They smell of old food, garbage, and something else I can't place.

Within moments, a sliver of light cuts through the shadows. As quickly as it appeared, it's gone, leaving Styx standing beside one of the nasty-smelling boxes.

She moves something over her shoulder and disappears in the next second.

Fuck!

Sticking my nose into the cold air, I sniff. "This way."

Chapter Twenty-One

Styx

W ITH MY CASH SOAKING in Borax, I twist my hair up into a knot on top of my head and stare into the sink. My mind keeps drifting to a pair of golden eyes framed by long, thick lashes that, if I'm being honest with myself, I'm completely envious of. Everything about that man screams 'fuck me!' and I am a very willing participant. Feather's rules be damned.

The last thing you need to be concerned with right now is sex. You have demons to hunt.

"You are such a catty bitch, you know that? Why must you rain on every wet dream I have?" I stalk out of the kitchenette and into my bathroom. Grabbing my toothbrush, I turn on the shower.

After a moment, that other voice decides to answer. *I'm being practical. Get a toy if you must, but keep your focus.*

Gah! "You make me sound like I am a succubus looking for her next victim!" I wail into the empty bathroom. Ever since my personality decided to split, I have not had a good dicking. Seriously. The bitch knows how to ruin the mood and lay a guilt trip as well as an Italian mother!

When the water is finally warm enough, I jump in and take the world's fastest shower. There are a lot of night owls in this building and the hot water goes fast. I dry off and slip into a clean pair of boy shorts and a tank that I left on the sink when Charon abducted me. With my hair wrapped in a towel, I go to rinse out my money. Literally laundering money is such a pain in the ass, but at least I don't have to worry about touching someone else's ass particles.

Before I reach the sink, I hear voices in the hallway outside my door. Not unusual for an apartment complex on the wrong side of town, but when I hear my name, I instantly go on high alert.

Slipping through the few shadows in my apartment, I grab Tod from his place on the wall. I quietly pull him from his sheath and make my way back to the front door in time to hear a muttered curse.

"Shh! She will hear you," comes a hushed masculine voice through the door.

"Damn right, she'll hear you! Who are you and what do you want?" I growl through the door. I probably should have waited to see what they—because there is obviously more than one of them out there—wanted before saying anything. Oh well.

The sound of flesh hitting flesh, followed by a low growl causes me to smirk while brandishing Tod, pointing his sharp blade to the door. "Styx...umm...can we...uhh...come in?"

I blow air between my lips, making them vibrate like a fart. "Oh, yes! Please, strange men in the middle of the night, come in! Are you fucking high?!" Not that I am afraid of them, with Tod, I can kill anything that comes through that door. The only reason I haven't swung it open and castrated them already is the curiosity that nags me. If I were a cat, I'd have been dead years ago.

"She's got you pegged," one of the men says with a chuckle.

"Fuck off, Ormr. Styx, it's Kyon. Please, let us in?"

Kyon? The Cerberus?

A shifter. Who'd have thought?

"Uhh...how in the hell are you fitting in my hallway??"

Raucous laughter echoes through the thin door. "I can shift, love," Kyon says after he's settled himself. "Now, before we scare your neighbors..." He trails off, leaving the question in the air.

"Don't make me regret this, kibble breath," I grumble as I unlock the door.

The two men...can they be considered men?...crowd in my kitchenette. The small space isn't very large, but it serves me well. However, with the two large males standing shoulder to shoulder, it looks more like a closet.

"All right. I let you in. Now what?" I plant my hands on my hips. Then drop them. Then fold them across my chest. Inside my head, I am screaming at myself because I feel awkward. Part of me...the pink, fleshy part between my legs...wants to climb Kyon like a sexy jungle gym. The logical part of me sees the giant dog who hangs out at the gates of Hell.

"Wait. Before you tell me why you are here, I want to know *how* you are here. I mean..." Indicating his burly, tall, normal...sexy, human body with a wave of my hand.

Kyon and his friend smile broadly. Both have such beautiful, straight, white teeth, and I swear a sparkle gleamed off one tooth with a mystical *ding*.

"We are shifters. Could you imagine a bunch of giant Cerberi walking around Hell all the time?" Kyon chuckles, the sound deep and erotogenic. Warmth rushes through me and I find myself waiting with bated breath for his next words...his next smile...hell, for his next breath!

"As for the why." Looking to his friend, Kyon seems to be suddenly at a loss for words. Eyes pleading.

"Kyon here is, umm. Well, he is a rare Cerberi. A hero among the rest of us," the other Cerberus states hesitantly.

"You came all this way to tell me that Kyon is your personal hero? Thanks for that. Can I go to bed now?" I ask, walking backwards towards the door, shooting my thumbs over my shoulder.

Kyon pushes his friend. "Ormr, you aren't helping." Turning to me, he sighs. "Styx, I'm just going to throw this out there and then you can do with it as you please. If that means you run me through with your sword, or you kick me out and never want to see me again, I'm going to be okay with that."

I have to admire his gumption; however, I have to admit his words put me on edge.

Sucking in a deep breath, Kyon's chest puffs up. "YouaremymateandIamheretoclaimyou," he rushes out in one long word.

Chapter Twenty-Two

Kyon

T HE WORDS RUSH OUT of me so quickly I'm not sure if she understands me.

Styx's red eyes widen, jaw drops. I hold my breath, waiting for her to swing her sword at me, punch me, or fall over laughing.

"Demon say what now?" She looks at me with a smirk before saying, "Are you going to piss on me?"

And with that comment, my hearts drop to the pit of my stomach. My shoulders droop, and I nod. Defeated.

"Good one, Styx," Ormr chuckles. I shoot him a glare. That's when Styx snorts, and when I look over, she has her hand over her mouth.

"Y-you are joking with me, right?" She snorts again. "Is this some kind of Cerberus-Demon hazing?" Her eyes alight with humor. I'm baffled.

"N-no. I'm—" I run my hands through my hair. "Styx, I didn't do this right. I should have plied you with pretty words or brought you flowers. That's what the humans do, yeah?"

Her smile falters. "You're serious." For a long moment, she stares at me. I can almost see her thought process in the minute flinches and ticks of the muscles in her face.

"This was a bad idea. Come on, Ormr, let's just go." I walk in the direction of the door, sidestepping Styx, and mumbling an apology as I pass. My face feels like it's on fire, my hearts—beating in tandem—feel as if they are breaking from her rejection.

Go back to her!

Show her the depth of our sincerity. She is ours!

My other sides argue, growl, and yell at me. For them, it is so easy with their mentality of egredere et vince. Go forth and conquer.

Take what is ours!

Make her see the truth of our hearts.

It doesn't work that way. I can't just club her over the head and drag her back to the Underworld. Not and expect her to stay with us in some warped happily ever after.

Worked for Hades.

Chapter Twenty-Three

Styx

K YON'S EYES LOSE THEIR spark, and his shoulders drop a degree. Guilt rages through me for putting the—pardon the pun—sad puppy dog look on his face.

I honestly thought it was something that Charon put the beast up to, you know...to fuck with me for being a bitch or something. If I'm being honest with myself, though, a part of me is elated that the sexy man wants me. And it goes beyond wanting his peen.

Oh, Zeus! Speaking of. What does his peen look like? Is it normal? Barbed? Spiked!? What about when he is in his dog form? Would I be expected to—

No. Nope. I don't mind freaky, but that is outside of my wheelhouse.

Am I really entertaining this? I've only ever had humans dip their wicks in me before, and the idea of what Kyon is hiding behind that zipper is making me drool.

"Kyon, wait." Blowing out between my lips, I wave for him to step away from the door. "I don't understand the whole mate claiming thing. How it works or why you think that I'm yours. I meet guys, get my pussy wet, and leave. This is a shock and extremely outside of my knowledge." I don't miss the vibrating growl that is emitting from his chest once I mention fucking other men.

"Give her the pretty words," Ormr stage whispers, nudging his friend.

Looking more uncomfortable than I feel, Kyon bashfully runs his hand through his hair. The action endears me to him even more.

Fine, I admit it. I wouldn't mind taking a roll in the proverbial hay with the Cerberus shifter. Not only has it been too long since I last had sex, but my curiosity is piqued.

"This isn't a normal thing for Cerberi to find their mates. Actually, it's practically unheard of. Usually, we are bred like...like humans breed dogs. The strongest of us are chosen when one of our females goes through her cycle."

"Her heat," Ormr adds in.

"Yea. Yes, her heat. The male and female are kept in a closed space that is large enough for the beasts, but comfortable enough for their 'human' forms. Once they've knotted, the female is tested for pregnancy."

"Woah! Wait. Hold your Night Mares. Are you telling me you are going to keep me locked in a room until you get me pregnant!? Heaven to the Hell NO! I will NOT be—"

Kyon's hands go up in a placating manner. "No, no! That is not what I'm saying at all. I swear. I just...I am messing this all up!" His brown wavy hair falls into his face as he hangs his head.

"What Kyon is badly trying to explain, lovely lady, is that the moment he first scented you sailing across with Charon, he knew there was something special about you. Something he wanted to know more about." Ormr graces me with that megawatt smile before continuing. "He went straight to Hades and Persephone and begged for them to allow him time Topside to find you."

"Oh-kay," I let the word drag out as Ormr's words circle around in my head.

"I feel it in both of my hearts. All of me knows that you are meant for me. They won't shut up about it, actually," Kyon chuckles.

"Both hearts? They?" I am riding the line between completely confused and utterly intrigued!

"My breed of Cerberi is the three-headed dog, as you know. Each has their own personality, and I hear them when I am in this form. And yes. Two hearts, and two stomachs when in Cerberus form." He takes a deep breath. "Styx, I don't expect you to drop everything. Not for me. I want you to get to know me. Decide for yourself if you accept my claim to you."

I stare at him, unblinking. That was a lot of information in such a short span of time. Seems I need anatomy lessons beyond where the peen goes. I know demons can look like just about anything, as devious and dark as the mind can conjure and then some. However, I never gave much thought to the innards.

Then, the whole mate claiming thing. What in the actual fuck am I supposed to say to that? How am I supposed to accept his heart...err...hearts, if I don't even know what is in my own? Am I capable of giving him more than a warm bed partner?

"Let's talk. I have questions. And I mean a *lot* of fucking questions. We could get some food. I always think better when I have bacon in my belly."

"Yes. I would like that." The fire is back in his golden eyes. Smaller, but there, nonetheless.

Chapter Twenty-Four

Kyon

S ITTING NEXT TO ORMR and across from Styx, I take in the delicious smells of the diner. I've never been to such a place, but she assures me they have all kinds of meats to enjoy.

Shortly after Styx tells the waitress all the things she wants brought to our table, her eyes—now a warm brown color due to the contacts she put in—search mine. We sit there staring at each other, neither of us flinching, blinking, or looking away. I feel as though she is digging deep into my very soul.

I hate the contacts because they make it feel like someone else is looking at me, and it's rather unnerving. I focus on the waves of emotions she's feeling trickling along my skin. Confusion, curiosity, and unease waft off her, all easy to detect. However, weaving between those is arousal and interest.

Trying not to get my hopes up about those latter emotions, I clear my throat. "What would you like to know?"

She cracks her neck, never taking her gaze from mine. "If Cerberi are not supposed to have 'fated mates,' how do you know I'm yours?"

I rub a fist over my hearts, trying my best to think of the words. "There is this ache that has been gripping me here. It started the moment I first saw your face break through fog. I thought it was curiosity, anxiety from meeting someone new. That is, until I spoke to Persephone."

"Hades' bitch, right?"

My eyes widen and I hear Ormr sucking in a breath of surprise. "You shouldn't speak of her that way! She is a goddess!" Ormr wheezes out.

"Sorry. I didn't mean it in a derogatory fashion. His woman. Better?" At our nods, she waves her hand for me to continue.

"Anyway, Persephone handed me a book about fated mates, rituals, experiences, and so on. I'm a *hound* for information and devoured the book's contents within the hour. Everything the book described, I felt."

Just as I finished speaking, the server brought over plates upon plates piled with food. None of the food looks familiar to me but it smells delicious.

"Bacon. Sausage. Ham. Those are eggs," Styx rattles off as she points to different things. "Hashbrowns, toast, and jam."

"What are the round fluffy things?" I ask, poking one with my finger.

A smile blooms across her lips. "Those are the best part. Pancakes." She grabs things off the various plates and puts them onto one of the empties. On the pancakes, she pours a thick, brown liquid she calls syrup.

After using her fork to cut off a piece of the pancake and syrup, she holds it out in front of my mouth. Unsure about the whole situation, I glance at Ormr who only shrugs.

"Take a bite. It's amazeballs!"

I lean closer to the fork and wrap my lips around it. The explosion of flavor crashes over my tongue and I close my eyes as I chew. A low purr rumbles from my chest.

"That was hot!" she exclaims.

I open my eyes quickly, looking around for whatever it is she is referring to. I swear, I have never been more confused in all my long life than I am around this demon.

"You. The purr. Damn! I want more of that! Here, try the bacon!" she urges.

Leaning closer to her outstretched hand, I keep my eyes on hers and watch as her pupils expand. I purposely accidentally flick my tongue over her thumb as I bring the piece of bacon into my mouth. Styx bites her lip and I growl.

Watching her watching me, I don't even register the taste of the bacon as I slowly crunch it between my teeth. Her gaze is glued to my closed mouth. When I swallow, she flicks her eyes to my throat, then back up to my mouth.

Deciding to take full advantage of this moment, I slip my tongue between my lips, licking away the grease. She mimics my actions, and my cock is instantly hard as fuck.

Noticing her hand is still held out over the table, I lean over and wrap my lips around her finger, intent on ridding the digit of the grease from the bacon.

Styx sucks in a breath as she squirms in her seat.

With my mouth occupied, I breathe in through my nose and the sweet aroma of her arousal travels through me like caressing hands.

Unholy Hades!

Chapter Twenty-Five

Styx

L ISTENING TO THE MAN purr over food makes me happy and horny. I want to leap over the table, food be damned—that's how much I want him, I'm willing to destroy food!

I am damn near destroyed when he pulls my finger between his soft, wet lips. His tongue twirls and rolls, massages the pad of my finger and I move my hips to try to ease the insane ache between my thighs. I think Kyon notices, but fuck it, he's the one sucking on my finger as if it's his life source!

His golden eyes burst with the flames of Hell, in their own way screaming his lust and desires. I watch as his nostrils twitch. His pupils blow out, obviously having taken in the new scent coming from between my thighs, my cropped shorts not acting as much of a barrier.

Yearning for more of the magic his mouth is creating, my ass leaves the chair as I lean further over the table. I gently pull my finger from his mouth, replacing it with my lips. With one hand on the table for balance and the other still gripped in Kyon's meaty fist, I lick at the seam of his lips, begging to enter.

It's the taste of him that is driving me wild. In addition to the syrup and bacon he recently consumed, his robust flavor bursts onto my tongue with each swipe. Warm apple pie...of all things.

Kyon's free hand wraps around the back of my neck and under my hair, pulling me even closer to him. I sidestep the table without taking my lips from his, then crawl into his lap. The clatter of plates and glasses as my ass bumps the table's edge barely registers.

Straddling his thick thighs, my toes press into the floor as I push my breasts against his chest. I dig both of my fingers into the thick curls at the base of his neck as his nails bite into my hips.

Kyon slides his hands up under my crop top. His calloused fingers smooth up my ribs and meet just below my tits. Sneaking his thumbs under my bra, he easily finds my nipples, which are stiff and sensitive due to his ministrations.

I lean back slightly, and rake my nails down his chest, over his abs, and to the button of his jeans.

A raucously loud throat clearing jars Kyon and I from the private bubble of lust we created around ourselves. We put a couple inches between our faces, turning to look at Ormr. I know the death glare I'm shooting our third wheel is responsible for the way he lowers his eyes.

"Hades below, Ormr!" I growl out.

"Public place. People are watching," he says quickly, still looking anywhere but at me. A quick glance over my shoulder validates Ormr's words as the handful of patrons quickly turn away.

I glance back at Kyon to find him playfully smirking back at me. "We can continue this conversation in private," he offers. His voice is velvet sex. Gone is the shy and unsure 'boy' of earlier, replaced by a man who knows what he wants and is willing to take it if need be.

Reaching into my back pocket, I pull out a small wad of cash. I hand it to Ormr and say, "Enjoy the food, don't forget to tip. See you back at my place in an hour." I look into Kyon's eyes when he squeezes my tits. Persephone's pomegranates! "Make it two."

Chapter Twenty-Six

Kyon

S TYX GRABS MY HAND, which I offer willingly, and storms out of the diner. A few of the humans left in our wake yelp out hoots and remarks such as, "Get it, girl!"

Once outside, she wastes no time dipping us into a pool of shadows. I expect her to push me against the wall and attack me with her mouth again. Instead, I feel twisted up as the shadow becomes impossibly dark. I can't tell if my eyes are open or closed. Then, suddenly, I'm blinded by the yellow light of the hallway of Styx's building.

"What the hell?"

"I shadow jumped. Quickest way to continue our...conversation." Styx tosses that out as if it is the most natural thing in the world while rushing up the stairs to her apartment.

Wasting no time, I take the steps two at a time. I am fully aware there is still a lot for us to discuss, but for the love of Hades and Persephone both, I can't find it in myself to care. Especially with Styx's ass bounding up the stairs in front of me.

Move faster!

Yes! Hurry! We want to taste our mate! My typically bickering other parts are in agreement for the first time in centuries. Our mate. I love the sound of that.

Finally, we are entering her small space. With a backwards kick, I close the door. Styx stands with her back towards me in her bedroom. She's putting her deadly sword in its sheath and removing the scabbard she has tied between her shoulder blades.

"Shut it," she growls out menacingly.

I turn to make sure I closed the door all the way. Yup. "It's closed."

"Oh, right. Good." She spins on her heel and holds her hands out to me. "Odd time to ask this...but, uh...do you have any STDs?"

I look at her quizzically. "I don't know what that is."

She laughs. "Have you ever had sex and gotten sick from it?"

"Oh! No. Cerberi don't get sick."

"Good. I don't think demons do, either. But I had to check. Safety and all. Still, we'll put on a condom." She fiddles around in a drawer and pulls out a small, foil square with the word 'Trojan' on it.

"What is that for?" I ask, eyeing the tiny package.

"Even though we can't get sick from each other...I could get pregnant. I don't know about you, but I'm so not ready for that responsibility." Styx puts the corner of the package between her teeth and pulls, successfully opening it.

"I, uh, have my own way of preventing pregnancy. As long as you are not in heat, and I don't knot inside of you, the only thing we will experience is each other's pleasure," I assure her as I step closer to her. Slowly stalking the demon female.

"We will talk about that knotting thing later," she commands.

"Of course," I oblige. My hands cup her face and I lean in, kissing her. She opens her lips right away, snaking her tongue out to wrestle with mine. Our saliva mingling and creating a new flavor all its own.

She drops her hands from my hips to the button of my jeans and deftly unlatches the bindings, allowing my hard as stone cock a little room to breathe. Tucked against my leg as it is, I will have to pull the jeans down to fully expose myself.

As her palm presses along the slightly swollen gland at the base of my cock, a delightful euphoria slams into me. My head falls back with a groan.

That's...

Yeah... my sides groan in unison.

Styx pushes my jeans down and my cock springs free, quickly followed by a gasp. Concerned, I snap my head down to look at her.

"This is...not to be rude, but...your dick is weird." A blush colors her beautiful cheeks as her eyes remain trained on the object at hand.

I'm about to apologize and remove myself from the situation when she wraps her hand around my cock. Her fingers don't touch her thumb, and then she adds her other hand. I wouldn't say she is caressing so much as exploring. She cups my balls with one hand while trailing her fingers over the ridge that spirals from just behind my knot to the tip of my penis.

"Talk about ribbed for my pleasure, huh?" she snickers. "What is this?" she asks, lightly massaging the small knot.

"That is what will keep you from getting pregnant. As long as I don't penetrate you to the hilt, it won't seal us together."

"So...if you *did* put all of you in me, you'd have to stay in me for..."

"Until the mating is complete. I thought you wanted to discuss this later?"

"Yeah. Definitely. I'm just. I've never seen a peen quite so beautiful and intricate before." She runs her wet tongue along her bottom lip. From her position on her knees, I can't see her entire face...pity...but I can feel her desire, can scent it on the air.

The list of things I want to do to her body grows longer with each moment that passes. Starting with tasting the delicacy she protects between her thighs. I want to commit her flavor and every inch of her body to mem—

"Hades belooowww," I exhale on a heated breath as she slides her tongue along, tracing the spiral ridge.

Chapter Twenty-Seven

Styx

H OT DAMN! I AM finally understanding what I have been missing by fucking humans all these years! As I run my tongue along the raised ridge that twirls around his peen, my jean shorts...not just my thong...become soaked. My pussy is throbbing, wanting to feel this monstrous cock inside of me.

The noises he makes as I explore are enough to drive me to orgasm. Deep growls vibrate from his chest to his dick, which is securely latched between my lips now. I swallow as I try to take as much of his length as possible. Another advantage to being a non-human, the fucker is hung like a damn horse! Makes sense, I suppose, considering the size of his Cerberus body.

The ridges bump along my tongue, the sensation both incredible and awkward. No, foreign.

What the hell are you doing? He is a damn dog. A gigantic dog! Get off your knees and throw him out!

Shut the fuck up! You are a part of me, and we need this. Besides, he isn't a dog right now!

This is ludicrous! You deserve better than this.

Maybe. But who are you to judge? You never want to have fun. Now shut up and let me enjoy myself!

Fuck! That bitchy, stick-in-the-mud part of me tries to ruin this experience. She keeps making snide remarks about getting fur in my mouth and giving birth to hellacious puppies.

Joke's on her, though. I honestly don't give a fuck. I need this to happen, I am not going to go unsatisfied...again...because of her.

Letting him fall from between my lips, I put my hands on his hips and pull myself to standing. He kisses my nose, my cheeks, and my forehead.

"Styx? Will you do me a favor?" he asks, his voice smokey sex.

"Hmm?"

"Take out your contacts. I want to see the real you."

I hold a finger up to him, indicating for him to wait one minute, then press it to his lips. The idea that someone wants to see me for all my demon glory—and won't go screaming into the hills—is a massive turn on. As if I needed help!

As quick as a flash, I'm in my little bathroom removing the brown contacts that I wear so the humans do not become unnerved. At the club, I can go without them. Between the darkness and the whole thrill the humans get from me being 'other' allows me to actually be me, even if they don't realize it.

Yet another benefit of being with Kyon. We both know what each other really is, two beings from the darkest depths of the Underworld. There is nothing to disguise, no secrets to keep. Just us, pleasure, and companionship. Even if we just use each other for the sex.

I slip out of my clothes, tossing them in the hamper, before returning to my bedroom and Kyon. He sits on my bed with his clothes off looking like a god of sex and desire. His toned abs, wide chest, muscular arms, and those thighs! There is something about a man with thick as fuck thighs that just kills me.

We've wasted so much time on talking, undressing, and staring. Not able to control myself any longer, damn thin patience, I practically pounce on him, pushing him to his back on the mattress. With a practiced hand, I slide the condom on his dick, a little surprised that it fits.

You're making a mistake.

Shut the fuck up!

I straddle his waist, rubbing my pussy against his long shaft as I kiss his neck. Kyon pulls my hair up with both hands, tying it, somehow, in a bun without a hair tie. With my neck now visible and obstruction free, he nuzzles my head to the side to give him better access.

As he drags his tongue in long strides up my neck, over my jaw, and to my temple, I groan. Rotating my hips a little to catch my clit against the ridges of his cock, my orgasm builds up in my abdomen. It's a delicious, heavy weight that is begging for release.

"I need..." he begins.

"Yeah," I pant, "me too." I grip his dick in my hand and line it up to my opening, hoping that I can take all of it. Well, except for the knot, that is. Humans...at least the ones I've been with...are not as endowed as the beast below me.

With a gentleness that belies his size and breed, Kyon eases his mammoth cock into me. The raised ridge seems more pronounced than it had in my mouth or hand. Maybe I'm just that much more sensitive. Each time the expanding ring of my pussy allows another ridge to pass, I shiver with delight.

I let Kyon guide me, more because I am concerned about that knot deal than any other reason. Taking in his length is a challenge that I am more than willing to take on...or *in* as the case is.

"Easy, my little flower," he whispers. I'm a little appalled at being called something so delicate and flimsy, but I still my movements, regardless.

"I need...to catch my breath. This is more than I ever could have imagined," he admits.

I try to judge how much more of him is waiting to plunge inside of me. I move one hand from his shoulder and slide it between us and wrap it around his shaft. It feels as if he is about halfway in, and my thighs quiver with excitement.

"Hades," he breathes out as he slowly pushes his hips up into me. He slides in deeper, the pressure making me feel full and unsure if I can possibly take anymore of him.

Then, he grips my hips and raises me up before thrusting into me a little faster. There isn't enough leverage for him to come out far enough before sliding back in place, and I feel his arms tremble slightly each time he lifts me. He is strong, but I think he is dividing his focus. He deserves to enjoy this as much as I do. So, I wrap my ankles behind his thighs, press my body to his, and roll so that I am on my back.

"Much better," he says as he continues to fuck me.

Although he isn't slamming into my pussy with vigor, the pace is perfect for the amount of peen that he is working with, my previously on edge orgasm topples over and I scream his name.

"Kyon!" That's more than one first for me. I've never come so quickly, nor have I ever used my lover's name.

My orgasm lasts longer than ever before as he continues to slowly massage my inner walls. Each time he is as far in as he dares to go, he growls deeply. The vibration is felt through my entire body, right down to my toes. If I were to die right now, I would go out a very happy little demon.

Chapter Twenty-Eight

Kyon

H ER HOT BREATH TICKLES my chest as I carefully inch my way into her inviting pussy. She's already come on my dick, but I still worry about the length of me hurting her. I know she can take it; she is strong, and she is a demon, but I've never had sex in my man form before.

When she comes again, cursing and panting my name, my fears subside. Albeit slightly. I pick up the pace, only delving in about halfway as her hips push upwards, working with me in tandem.

A strong tingle in my spine alerts me to the upcoming orgasm. As it rides through me, I press in closer to her. Nuzzling her chin so she turns her head to the side, I lick at her neck. Trail my tongue from her collar bone to the back of her ear over and over again, committing her pheromones to memory. She reminds me of the delicate flowers in my greenhouse, although she is anything but delicate.

"I'm going to—FUCK! Kyooonnn!"

As she belts out her orgasm, mine follows suit, and that is when I strike. I bite down on the soft flesh where her neck and shoulder meet. The spicy tang of her blood washes over my tongue.

MINE!

MINE!

OURS! I correct them as I claim our little heart fire for ourselves. Out loud, though, as I lick at the wound I've inflicted on her, I say, "Mine."

Chapter Twenty-Nine

Styx

"**M**ine," he growls in my ear as he licks a patch of my neck that is now stinging deliciously.

In my euphoric state of complete and utter satisfaction, I just lie there with my eyes closed and smile contently. Fuck it. Let the sexy beast claim me. If he can screw me into this kind of bliss, he's worth keeping around. As long as he's housebroken. I chuckle at my private joke.

"What's so funny?" Kyon asks tiredly from his sprawled-out position next to me.

"N-nothing," I snicker. "Private joke."

He looks at me from under his thick lashes, his golden eyes simmering after having been enflamed all this time. What a fucking sexy glow to bask in! Yeah, waking up to that every morn—

"Wait a minute! You bit me! You claimed me, didn't you??"

Kyon has the decency to look a tiny bit guilty, but the balls to look aphrodisiacal while doing it. "I couldn't resist it. I can't resist you. Deep inside of me, I know that you are the only creature I am meant to lie with. Tell me you don't feel a connection to me. Tell me and I will walk away, relishing only in this stolen moment of time for the rest of my days."

His words, and more importantly, his sincerity wash over me. He isn't just looking for a wet vessel to stick his junk into, he is looking for someone to complete his heart. And, according to him, that someone is me.

Words. It's all just words to trap you. I can't believe you had sex with him, and now you are listening to his drivel.

I've told you before, get the stick out of your ass already. Live a little, you crotchety old bitch!

Maybe he is telling me what he thinks I want to hear. But why would he give me the pretty words after he already fucked me? He got what he wanted. Heh...we both did.

I sit up, turning towards Kyon and criss crossing my legs. "We need to talk." Pushing the bits of hair that have slipped from the knot, that is surprisingly still intact, behind my ears. "Are you feeding me bullshit? Be honest with me."

Kyon mirrors my position and puts his hands on my knees, his thumbs drawing slow circles on my skin. "My little flower, there are few things I cannot do. I am unable to travel Topside without permission, I can't figure out how to grow an orchid." With that declaration, he gifts me with the cutest embarrassed smile. "And I cannot lie."

"I am going to tackle those one at a time. One, what would happen if I accept your claim, then? Would I have to relocate to Hell?"

"That would be a discussion to be had with my lords Hades and Persephone."

"Okay. We will put a tack in that one for now. Two. Orchids? Really?"

"Thanks to Charon, I have grown quite fond of what humans call 'nature.' Persephone, Goddess of Harvest and Fertility, helped me create a greenhouse in the Underworld. Orchids are temperamental and difficult to grow. Charon brought me one once, but it died before he could give it to me. Shame. I bet it was stunning." A sincere passion for agriculture and life brims in his eyes.

"I don't know anything about that, but it sounds like a pain in the ass." Kyon nods. "And you can't lie? As in, if I ask you if my ass looks big in this dress, you will tell me it does?"

"Your ass is perfect no matter what type of cloth you put over it. However, yes. If you were to ask me a question, I cannot lie to you. Ever. Ask me anything."

Biting the inside of my bottom lip, I study his face for any twitches or tells as I think of something to ask him. He doesn't know things I would know and vice versa, so how do I even tell if he is lying or not?

My inner bitch sighs dramatically. *Ask him something you already know the answer to. Gauge his facial expressions on that.*

"Did you like when I had your dick in my mouth?" No one ever accused me of being subtle.

His eyes flame up slightly, his lips twitch at the corners. "Very much so."

"How old are you?"

"Two-thousand-eight-hundred and forty-nine. Or nearly three millennia."

My jaw drops and my eyes feel like they are bugging out of my head. "Damn! You look fucking incredible for an old man." I wink.

Wow. Did I just wink at him?

You did. If he is that old, and, as Charon said, the beast is the top Cerberi...

...your point?

My point is that he said the best Cerberi are bred. He probably has kids or a mate. And you are just spreading your legs for him. That cunty voice chuffs.

"Kids."

"What about them?"

"Do you have any?"

"I sired thirteen. All of whom are part of the Cerberi pack. They help protect the Underworld, the souls, and Hades and Persephone. My daughters, there are three, are Persephone's personal guards. I would love for you to meet them," Kyon's eyes light up in a different way when talking about his...kids? Pups?

"What of their mother?" A deep-rooted pang of jealousy spikes through me.

"Mothers," he corrects, and my body heats with anger. "Little flower, as much as I love my pups, their mothers and I were bred. There was no emotional attachment there. It was part of our duties to populate the pack. Nothing more."

Mulling over his words, his confessions, I realize that I very much want to meet his pups. But... "If I become your fated mate, I couldn't give you Cerberi babies. They'd be half breeds. Let's be honest, I don't want to share you with another female, either."

"Another question for Hades and Persephone. I *believe* that part of my duties would be null and void, considering our connection." That eases my mind...slightly.

"Would you still want to breed with other Cerberi?"

"No." His answer is as solid as a rock and quick.

"I will make you a deal. Let me get my questions answered by Hades and Persephone. If what they say jibes with me, you and I will discuss this fated mate thing." Am I really considering this? I've known the mutt for less than forty-eight hours, the man for less than ten.

"One more question, before you answer that. Do you love me?"

"As drawn to you as I am, I believe that to love you would be to know you. I *can* say that I love your smile, and the look you get in your sparkling ruby eyes when you are about to come or when you are teasing me." A broad smile stretches across his lips.

"I can respect that," I reply honestly.

"Ask me instead if I believe that I *will* love you."

"Okay. Do you believe that someday you will love me?"

"Persephone once told me that I was blessed by the Goddess of Love herself, Aphrodite. Which is why I have been *allowed* to find you, to find my truest mate. Although, because it's unprecedented, there are a lot of...walls to break through. So, yes, my little flower, I believe I will love you. Whole-heartedly."

Chapter Thirty

Kyon

A FTER MY CONFESSION, STYX kind of just...stares at me. I wish I could read her mind right now to know where her mind is going with everything. She offered to hold court with Hades and Persephone to determine what out future would look like, which tells me she is at least strongly considering my proposition.

I readily agree to her terms and wait while she takes a shower.

As she closes the bathroom door, three taps sound on the front door. Ormr has returned, I pick up his scent as I stand from my lounging on the bed.

"Is it safe?" he asks, poking his hand through the open doorway, shaking a bag full of food like a white flag.

"She's in the shower, as if you can't hear her." All Cerberi are gifted with a strong sense of smell and equally strong hearing.

"Yes, yes." He waves my comment away. Sniffing the air pointedly, he grins. "So, she's accepted you, eh?"

I run down the briefest possible version of my conversation with my little flower. After explaining her request to seek further information from our lords, Ormr nudges his cheek against mine.

"I'm happy for you, brother. This went more smoothly than I imagined it would," he admits.

I pick through the bag of food as Ormr goes on about the diner and the interesting people he talked to there.

"There was a group of females there talking about monster peens in romance books. They were a lively bunch. Delaney was telling them about suction cup penises on aliens, and then the others were chiming in. Becca suggested they were on the foreskin, while Mel argued that it would have to be near the base." Ormr and I laugh.

"Humans. If only they knew what lurks in the shadows. Ammiright?" Styx interjects.

Ormr and I turn to look at her and my jaw drops. She is wearing leather pants that hug every single curve. Her dark hair hangs down her back in soft curls, and her lips are the exact shade of red as her eyes. But the crème de la crème is the black tank top stretching across her ample breasts that says, 'The Devil is a loser and he's my bitch.' Along the side of the words is a red devil with a long tail that ends on an arrowhead styled point.

"That is what you're going to wear to meet the God of the Underworld and his bride?" I ask incredulously.

"It's scandalous." Ormr smirks.

"He is just another demon, you know."

"Actually, he is not 'just another demon.' He is the god of the Underworld!" I exclaim. It bothers me that she doesn't show the respect for Hades that he deserves. I've gleaned from the millennia I've spent with souls how much they fear Hades. The humans on Topside think he is an evil god who terrorizes the souls sent to him. I can't recall how many times I have growled at souls for bad mouthing my lord.

"Okay. Okay! I won't insult him," she concedes, "but I'm not changing. If Hades wants to know me, he will know the kind of demon I am."

"Deal. We should go."

"Back so soon?" Charon asks as he greets us on the shore of the River Acheron. From there he will take us across the Marshes of the Styx to get to Hades' palace.

"Hey, old demon. I'm going to meet with Hades and Persephone. Make sure Sparky doesn't bite me this time, yeah?" Styx waits for me to step into Charon's skiff and hold my hand out to her.

"Oh, to be a fly on the wall for that conversation," Charon chortles. Once Ormr is situated, Charon uses his staff and pushes away from the shore.

As we move through the marsh, Styx looks around, watching the craggy scenery go by. She is curious about everything, and I find it enchanting. Sadly, the ride is over too soon. I would have been fine sailing around and watching the toasty air of the Underworld pushing through her hair with its scorched fingers. The hellfire reflecting in her eyes is quite possibly the sexiest sight I've ever witnessed.

"Here we stop. Make sure you tell me everything!" Charon crows as we walk away from his skiff. His cackle follows us as we move up the path to Hades and Persephone's home.

One of my daughters is curled up along the path in front of the palace. Her mane of hissing snakes slither awake as her right eye slits open. She is perfectly trained, thank you very much, so her faux sleep is part of the ruse. That false sense of security is meant to lure and distract.

"Who is that?" Styx asks, pointing at the Cerberi on the lawn.

"This," I say as we step up to my pup. "Is my daughter, Cressida." At the sound of my voice, the snakes reach out towards me happily.

Cressida sits up, and I step up to her, nuzzling my cheek against her lowered muzzle. "You can shift, love. I want you to meet someone."

Shimmering heat with a touch of mist surrounds her beastly dog-like body, giving way to Cress in her female bi-ped form. She stands about six feet tall, muscular yet lean. Her brown hair, much like my own, hangs to her chin, her gray eyes—a gift from her dam—are sharp, taking in everything.

"Cressida, this is Styx. Styx, my oldest daughter, Cressida. She is Persephone's number one." I want to continue praising my pup. Not because I think I need to put her on a pedestal for Styx, but because I don't know what else to say.

"It's nice to meet you, Cressida. Your Cerberus side is intimidating. You know, in the gorgeous beast kind of way," Styx says with class and not a hint of fear for the beast that Cressida is in both of her forms.

"Pleasure. Diggin' the shirt. Very badass!" Cress replies. Being as close to Persephone as she is, she has picked up more about Topside language than I have.

"Are Hades and Persephone around, love?"

"Sure, Dad. Inside. Ormr, tell me about your trip while they go and do the adulting," Cress coos.

Chapter Thirty-One

Styx

"Are Ormr and Cressida a thing?" I ask once we climb the stone stairs to the front door.

"Not that I'm aware of," Kyon says with uncertainty as he looks back with furrowed brows. I've seen that look on Feather's face when her protective instincts would take over at the club. That watchful eye that only those who truly love you can master.

"Well, I wouldn't worry about it. You said Cerberi don't do the whole bonding thing, right?"

"They can bond, but it isn't the same as fated mates. Although we are hell beasts, we can still love." Kyon sounds a little offended.

Yeah, okay. A *lot* offended.

He knows I don't know anything but what he's told me about his kind, so I chalk it up to him being nervous.

Before I can explain that I didn't mean to insult him or his daughter, he pulls on a cord to the side of the ornately carved stone door. One would have to be strong as fuck to open the damn thing. Unless there's some kind of magic involved.

Moments later, a squat, toad-like demon opens the door to us. He...I assume...speaks in a form of demonic I'm not familiar with. Of course, I only know some demon tongue, but this dialect is über foreign to me.

Kyon responds to him in the same language and the demon ushers us inside. "Apparently, Hades has been expecting us."

"That doesn't sound too foreboding," I utter sarcastically.

We follow the demon with the forked tail through the elaborate mansion. His stride is short, but he makes up for it with speed. Trying not to show how interested I am in the furnishings and decorations; I instead study the swishing of the demon's tail.

"We are to wait in this room, my lords will be here shortly," Kyon explains after more demon talk. He wraps his arm protectively around me, pulling me close to his back as he enters the room. Sticking his nose in the air, he deeply inhales. Seemingly satisfied, he brings me into the room.

A sharp intake of breath startles me. More so when I realize it came from my own mouth. It's a library. No, not just a library...this room puts the one in Beast's castle to shame! An absolute treasure trove of knowledge! Maybe being a resident of Hell wouldn't be *so* bad.

"This is one of my favorite places in the Underworld," my protective Cerberus beams whimsically.

Your *Cerberus?* My not-so-quiet other self snarks.

Wait. What? I didn't say that.

No. But you thought it. Bad idea, Styx. Very bad idea.

Bite me.

"Styx?" His tone tells me this isn't the first time he's called my name.

"Yeah?"

"I was asking what you think of the library."

"It's beautiful. No, it's incredible! I can see why you love it so much."

"When we are finished here, I want to show you my very favorite place." Kyon smiles at me, the flame is back in his eyes. "Of course, it is easily becoming my second favorite place." His smirk is sexy, and I can only assume to what—or should I say where—he is implying.

"You can scratch that itch later, Kyon," a deep, jovial male voice pulls me from gazing into Kyon's eyes, imagining looking at those eyes while he is between my thighs.

I turn towards the doorway, standing there is a tall man with dark hair and brooding dark eyes. He is wearing a white t-shirt—yeah, I'm shocked at that too—that shows off his massive, tattooed arms. Most noticeable are the intricate keys that seem to encircle his left wrist. His dark jeans hang nicely off his hips, ending at scuffed work boots.

"Lord Hades!" Kyon greets him with a low bow. When he stands, he grasps my hand. "I introduce you to Styx, the demon who calls to my heart." His comment makes my heart stutter and for the first time in my life, I feel a blush color my cheeks. How human!?

"Styx, it is a pleasure to meet you formally. However, I won't be your bitch." Although his tone is neutral, I'm flabbergasted and confused at his remark. He must sense that because he nods towards my shirt.

"OH! Right. Yeah, about that..."

"No need to explain yourself. Charon has told me that you are a...what were his words? Oh, yes, a 'Grade A pain in the ass.'" With this, Hades chuckles, eliciting a laugh from Kyon, too.

"Yup. That's what he told me, too. She is spirited, for sure."

"At least it was a great ice breaker," I offer with a shrug.

"That it was. My darling Persephone will be joining us momentarily. Until then, may I offer a drink?" Hades playing grand host. The god is surprising.

"Isn't there some...rule to not eat or drink anything in the Underworld?" I mean, isn't that how Persephone got sucked into staying down here?

Hades grins, a slightly terrifying sight. "It would be, but you were born here. That makes you exempt."

I nod, unsure what to say.

"Hades, you'd better not be tormenting our guest!" The musical voice is stern and still intensely enchanting. A breath later, Persephone glides into the library. Her long red hair flows over her shoulders and hangs to her hips. The color seems to emphasize her creamy white skin and delicate features. In contrast to Hades 'work attire,' she is stylish but comfortable in a long maxi dress.

"Lady Persephone." Kyon repeats his low bow. "I present to you the demon Styx, who calls to my heart."

"You are just as captivating as Kyon described!" Persephone says as she takes both of my hands, stretching my arms out to the sides as she looks me over. I suspect this is how a mother would react to her prospective daughter-in-law. "The shirt! I'm just seeing the shirt! I need to get one," she stage whispers with a wink.

"I'm not liking the shirt anymore," Hades groans playfully.

After a few more teasing words, we are invited to sit in the large leather chairs in the center of the room. The chairs are situated in a loose circle, so they all face one another. Kyon sits to my left, Persephone to my right, leaving Hades across from me.

Everyone is watching me, it seems. I slip a hand between the soft leather and my leg so I can discreetly dig my nails into my thigh. Put me in a roomful of men staring at me while I dance in next to nothing and I'm fine. Confident. But having two deities watching every move, or non move, I make is killing me.

"I claimed her during the most intense orgasm I have ever had, but she has questions before she will accept," Kyon blurts out, breaking the silence. His statement might have embarrassed a human, or even a demurer demon...if there is such a thing. Not me, though. We are all adults here. Even if I am the youngest by a couple millennia.

"I would be surprised if she *didn't* have questions," Persephone responds.

"Ask away," Hades invites.

"If I accept his claim, will I have to relocate here? What of his responsibility here? To you?"

The king and queen of the Underworld look at each other as if they are discussing my questions in private.

After an agonizingly long twenty-six seconds, they seem to have concluded their conversation. Persephone smiles warmly but doesn't say anything. I'm sure she has great sway over her husband, but at the end of the day, Kyon is *his* Cerberus.

"We believe that you and Kyon, should you complete the mating, can and will decide what is best for you both. As sad as I would be to lose him—if he chooses to join you Topside—I know that he would be doing so for the very best reason."

"We would love for you to visit as often as possible, though." That beautiful smile is friendly and sincere. I feel a connection to this goddess as if we could be true friends.

"What of the souls? The gate?" Kyon asks.

"Kyon, you have sired and trained thirteen amazing Cerberi. Not to mention the dozens of others you've trained throughout your service. Any one of your sons would take up the mantle with pride and precision," Hades offers. "You have served your entire life as the Guardian of the Underworld. I think you deserve to retire."

Chapter Thirty-Two

Kyon

W ITH THEIR BLESSING, I feel a little better about leaving my post. I know that my new destiny includes my mate, but after two and a half millennia of guarding the gates of the Underworld, the old adage comes to mind; 'you can't teach old dogs new tricks.' What if I can't make it Topside? How do I know I'll be able to control my shift?

"Kyon? You're looking a bit green over there. Are you okay?" Styx asks, reaching over to grip my arm.

I look at her hand, my eyes trailing up her arm to her concerned face. There is a softness in her red eyes that brings a smile to my heart. Even if she hasn't confirmed her acceptance, she is my mate and she is concerned for me.

"In all honesty, I'm nervous about my ability to survive Topside."

"Can't teach an old dog new tricks, huh?" she teases, throwing my thoughts at me.

"Exactly."

"You are not alone here. I'm going to have to learn how to live with another being. One who will be sharing my bed. We will get through this. Together." She smiles at me with an uneasy confidence.

Wait. Did she just...?

My eyes widen as it hits me. She's accepted the mating! I leap from my seat and drop to my knees in front of her. My hands slide along her jaw and into her hair, pulling her towards me. Kissing her, I pour every ounce of gratitude, happiness, and arousal that is filling my soul into each pass of my tongue.

As her tongue clashes with mine, all of her emotions are pushing into me. Her need, her own arousal, and her determination. Her hands have found their way into my hair, nails scoring my scalp in a deliciously painful way.

Styx is mine and I am hers from now until life is no more. And then some!

Hades clears his throat loudly and with emphasis. I'm pretty sure it isn't the first time, either. "There are still matters to discuss."

I pull Styx from her chair and turn so I can take her now empty seat, pulling her to curl in my lap. "Of course, My Lord," I say. "My apologies for being inconsiderate. "

"Kyon, there is no need to apologize! You've just had your claim accepted. If these matters were not important, we would leave you to celebrate properly." Persephone, always the sentimental one, smiles with tears brimming her lashes.

"First," Hades begins, "congratulations to you both. We will have a proper ceremony as soon as possible. Which brings me to the next order of business." He looks directly at Styx, his deep brown eyes flaring with the flames of the Underworld as he uses his godly powers. I've seen this studious glare before on many occasions to know what he is doing. While my beasts are growling inside my head at the intensity of his gaze on our mate, we keep it to ourselves. This is our master, after all.

Styx is fidgety, but she holds her own. Her soul is shaking under the weight of Hades' stare, I can feel it in my bones. Part of my Cerberus talents.

"Your sword is your destiny. It is not merely silver and copper, it's been magicked to be a prison." Hades' words resonate with power. "Although I have an affinity for precious metals, I cannot unlock the cell. Therein lies *your* destiny, Styx."

Flabbergasted, Styx stammers, "I-I don't have the ability to...to...free whatever being is trapped in Tod! I'm a hunter. A stripper. I don't have magic!"

"Of course, you do," Persephone soothes. "All creatures of the Underworld have some form of magic. The trick is unveiling it."

"With all due respect...how in Hades' hairy balls am I supposed to do that!?"

Chapter Thirty-Three

Styx

P ERSEPHONE TRIES TO HIDE a smile behind her hand, but the shoulder shaking gives her away.

"I'll have you know that I meticulously shave my balls." Hades' tone is serious and slightly insulted. I can't help but guffaw in shock!

Once I'm able to control my laughter, I try a different approach. "Okay...well, how in Charon's hairy balls am I supposed to break the magic. I'm only a demon. I don't possess the gifts of the gods."

Chuckles surround me as I poke fun at the ancient ferryman.

"You *do* weild god-like gifts, my little flower. The shadow jumping," Kyon offers.

"Shadow jumping?" Hades asks in surprise. "Explain."

"I can move within shadows." I shrug. "I pull them around me and am able to move to another location within seconds, depending how far apart they are. If I am going where I have not been before, the shadows...call to me, direct me where to go."

Hades looks over to Persephone with a raised brow. "Sound familiar?"

"Could it be? I mean...that would have had to happen..." Persephone looks to me. "How old are you, dear?"

"Uh...well, by my best calculations, I am around twenty-seven," I answer as honestly as possible.

"The timing is about right," the goddess whispers as she chews on her lower lip.

"I like you, Persephone. I do. But if you don't start filling me in about whatever this is, I can't promise that I will be a very pleasant guest." I cross my arms over my chest and rest them on Kyon's, which are wrapped around my waist.

"Please, understand, Styx," Persephone begins. "If we are correct in our assumptions, this news can be upsetting. However, I think it is incredibly important for you to know what your heritage is. Regardless of repercussions."

"I agree. Perhaps we should call for a meeting." Hades stands, steps behind the chair his wife is occupying, and begins to rub her shoulders.

"If it makes any difference to you, Charon thought he had some insight. Perhaps we should talk with him first?" I offer with a tilt of my head. "He seemed wary to—pardon the pun—rock the boat."

"On it." The lord of the underworld leaves the room.

"While we wait, Kyon, why don't you bring Styx to the kitchen and find something to eat? It's safe, I promise."

"Thank you for your hospitality, but I really don't feel like eating at the moment. I have spent many years wondering who my parents were and questioning why they abandoned me. My stomach can't handle the nerves." I haven't spoken so candidly about my true emotions regarding my parents in a long time. After waiting so long, I didn't see the point in letting it rent space in my mind any longer.

"I can respect that."

The three of us sit quietly, none of us sure of what to say as we wait for Hades to return. Persephone walks over to one of the many bookshelves and chooses a tome. She leafs through it as if looking for where she left off. The motion seems natural, telling me she spends a lot of time enjoying these books. I envy that. I've always wanted to read book, after book, after book.

Kyon rubs his hands up and down my arms. He doesn't utter a word, but I swear I can feel his thoughts. Not with precision, but enough to understand he is nervous and excited. Okay, so maybe that is more a feeling his emotions kind of thing, but either way.

Not being able to stand the silence any longer, I decide to ask some questions about the bond and what it means. Hades doesn't have to be present for that, at least.

"So, what all does a fated mating bond entail?"

Persephone sets down her book and returns to her seat. "A fated mate, as you can probably guess, is exactly what it sounds like. Sometimes it is a couple chosen by the Fates, sometimes by gods or goddesses. Regardless, someone decided somewhere down the line that you and Kyon are destined to be together."

"Whether we like it or not?"

"That doesn't usually play into their plans. However, there have been instances of rejected mates. Those very rarely end well for the couple in question."

"And the bond? Will we be able to have discussions telepathically like you and Hades were doing before?"

A blush tickles the goddess' cheeks. "That is a typical bonus to the bond, yes. There are situations where the bonded couple are able to...harness each other's powers or gifts. However, with Kyon being a Cerberi, it is uncertain. At least, I personally do not know what to expect."

Kyon shifts beneath me a little. "Do you know anyone who may know?"

Persephone chews on her lip some more, looking up at the high ceiling for answers. After a moment, she says, "It is possible that the Fates may know."

Great. Another faction I have to meet with for answers before I can get on with my life. Perhaps by the time this is all said and done, I will have a complete family tree and the ability to shift for all I know.

"If Kyon chooses to live Topside, how will that work? I mean, he doesn't have papers, he won't be able to shift..."

"Papers are easy enough to get. As for shifting, if the need becomes too strong, you can both come down here for a visit. I'm sure you will want to check in with your pups, anyway, right?"

"Definitely. I've never gone long without seeing them. It would break my heart to start now. I don't care how old they are, they will always be my babies," Kyon says with absolute pride.

A pang. No, it's more like a deluge of jealousy coursing through me, making my blood boil. It doesn't happen as much as it used to, but unholy hell, that hurts! Suddenly, I am unable to breathe. I feel like a hellhound is sitting on my chest and tearing at my lungs!

Heat blooms through me and I fight Kyon as I try to get off his lap. He is too close. His heat isn't helping me. I need to get away. I need to breathe. I need air. I need this pain to go away.

Fire. I'm engulfed in invisible flames. My lungs scorching. My heart burning, shriveling. My blood boils.

HELP ME! I scream. It must be only in my head because my tongue is charcoal in my mouth.

STYX! OPEN YOUR EYES! Take control of your breathing! I swear to you, you are not on fire. This is all in your head. Come on now, girl! BREATHE, DAMNIT!

That soft song begins to rattle through my head. It breaks through the fire. It breathes life back into my scorched body. It rejuvenates my soul.

My lungs fill with fresh oxygen, but they ache. The lullaby I've always heard in my dreams. It is saving my life. It kickstarts my heart.

Within moments, I'm breathing normally again. The weight is off my chest. I barely open my eyes and the light is diminished compared to the fire I swore was surrounding me seconds ago.

"Little flower, come on now, love. Breathe for me. That's it." Kyon's strong voice breaks through the soft lullaby. "I've got you. You're safe. Breathe out now. That's a good girl."

I open my eyes to see Kyon's golden ones aflame with panic, despite how calm his tone is. The crinkles at the corners tell me he is smiling now that my eyes are open. There is something...strange about his hair. It's hanging towards me. A quick glance around and I realize I'm on the floor.

"What?" I croak.

"I believe you had a severe panic attack," the soft, motherly voice of Persephone answers me as Kyon lifts me onto his lap. He situates me so my back is against his chest.

"You were having trouble breathing and then you were screaming about a fire burning you from the inside out. You hurt your throat, screaming the way you were." My mate—yes, I am comfortable with that term now—sounds close to tears and my heart aches as guilt once again crashes into me.

"I'm so sorry I worried you, mate."

"My heart's fire, it is not your fault that you...you called me mate," he breathes out the last part.

All I can do is turn in his lap and smile at him before he crashes his mouth against mine.

This is what it feels like to be loved, Kyon's voice breaches my mind, and I pull back with a gasp.

Chapter Thirty-Four

Kyon

"I just heard you. In my head!" Styx exclaims with wide eyes and a beaming smile.

"Really? Try again," I urge. *You have a beautiful smile.*

"You think I have a beautiful smile? Can you hear me?"

I want to feel you inside me again. Soon!

Her voice in my mind is heavy with desire and I'm instantly hard.

"I guess so." She giggles, stops herself abruptly, and clears her throat. I have a feeling she doesn't giggle very often, if at all. If that's the case, then I should feel damn proud that I elicited that response from her.

"Charon will be here within moments." Hades stops and takes in the room. "What did I miss?"

Persephone moves to his side and places delicate and excited hands on his forearm. "They can communicate telepathically! Isn't it wonderful? They're bonding!" she coos like a proud mama.

"Congratulations! One question with an answer, only a googolplex to go," he teases.

One minor step in the grand scheme of things, but I'll take it happily and willingly. Although we haven't discussed her past where other men are concerned, I know I am not her first. But that giggle, even cut short, I know within my soul that I am the first to receive that little treasure from Styx.

Thinking of ways I can make her giggle more often—I can't help myself, it's an adorable noise—I am interrupted by Charon's plume of smoke.

"'Sup, old timer?" Styx greets the ferryman with a raise of her chin. I marvel at how easily she switches gears, but even more so that she dares speak that way to someone as revered and ancient as Charon.

With a roll of his eyes, he seems to ignore Styx's comment. He would sell his intention more had he been able to hide the tiny smirk. He has grown to like her, even if just a few bars above tolerance. Perhaps it's the way she speaks to him without fear, treating him like everyone else.

My millennia of friendship with Charon has taught me much about the minor god. His task of bringing souls from Topside to their earned afterlives has left him lonely and feared. Most of the other Cerberi have a professional relationship with Charon, just the way he claims to like it. But I know him better than that, and I can tell he has subconsciously let Styx into his inner circle.

"Charon, we appreciate you joining us on such short notice." Hades magicks a fifth chair among the others. "I assume you know why I asked you here?"

"Yes, Lord Hades. Our newest pain is quite the conundrum, is she not?" Charon smiles warmly at the demon in question.

"That 'pain' is more than a conundrum. Styx is Kyon's bonded mate and an honorary member of this family." Persephone, usually quite calm and peaceful, exudes a muted version of fierce protectiveness over my mate.

Is she...angry with Charon? Over me?? she asks along our newly formed bond.

Yes, my little flower. The goddess has claimed you as one of her own. I can't keep the pride and gratitude from seeping into my words. She has made quite the impression, apparently, on the Queen of the Underworld.

"I mean no disrespect, My Lady." Charon bows deeply. "I think Styx is a fine demon bathed in mystery and intrigue. You know how much I love a good puzzle," he winks.

Persephone smiles, turns to Styx. "How about we figure out your heritage?"

Styx's emotions swirl around my heart and I curl up to her back, snaking my arms around her. *Breathe, my heart's fire. We don't know anything yet.*

I can't face them, she all but whimpers.

You don't have to. I believe Hades, Persephone, and Charon want to know so they can better understand what you are capable of. It could be imperative to solving this whole sword-prison thing.

Tight-lipped, she nods. Her small nails bite into my forearms.

"Do you really think she could have hidden that? I mean, that is a pretty hefty secret," Hades asks, and by the sound of things, I missed part of the conversation.

"Considering her gifts, I believe it is quite possible. Even from your all-seeing eyes." Charon concedes.

"How can we find out without offending her or her husband?" Persephone asks delicately.

The three of them seem to all go into a fugue state as they think.

My mind is overrun by flashes of memories. They aren't mine, though. Tilting my head, I close my eyes. I try to grasp just one memory as they zoom by.

THERE!

A woman—obvious by the shape of her body—in a hooded cloak carefully steps out of a pool of shadows. Her face is covered in shadows cast by the size of the hood. She's carrying something. Then she looks my way. On instinct, I inhale slowly and deeply, hunting for her scent.

A mixture of at least two familiar aromas waft across my olfactory senses. One more prominent and zips straight to my heart. The other tickles my brain, but I can't quite place it.

"Styx," I whisper.

The woman startles and looks at me. Like *really* looks at me. Her hand goes to her shrouded face before she steps back into the shadows and disappears.

"Kyon!?"

Panic punches through the vision. My mate is panicking.

Shaking my head, I am brought back to the here and now. What in the name of Hades is going on here?

Chapter Thirty-Five

Styx

K YON WHISPERS MY NAME, but when I turn to look at him over my shoulder, his eyes are scrunched closed. His eyebrows are arrowed down in...confusion? Pain? I can't tell which. I call his name three times without a response. Panicking, I yell, "Kyon!?"

He steps away from me and shakes his head quite literally like a dog. His eyelids pop open and concern etches the skin around his golden eyes. "My heart's fire, are you all right?" he asks.

"Me? I'm fine. Where did you go? I couldn't feel you," I tell him, rubbing my palm over my heart.

"I had a weird...vision. Hades, why did I have a vision? I don't have visions!" Kyon sounds positively freaked out.

"Explain what you saw, Kyon." Hades pulls Kyon—and by extension, me—to a chair.

Kyon explains in great detail what he saw, and I meet Charon's gaze. His recounting is spot on from what I saw when I first met Charon. The heat rises in my chest again.

"That was a memory, one of Styx's to be exact," Charon attests. "Curious."

"Elaborate, please." Hades does not look like he is very interested in beating around the bush.

Charon gives a short version of the vision that we both experienced. "It seems that their bond is stronger than only telepathic abilities. The memory you encountered is what I believe to be Styx's mom squirreling her away from the Underworld."

"She...me? What?" I had no idea that Charon thought that. Why didn't I pick up on that? "How can that be a memory? Especially from the point of view of an outsider?" I query. I'm confused, utterly lost.

"I have a theory," Charon begins.

"The shadows?" Hades asks, his eyes wide with surprise, and Charon nods.

"Paint the picture a little faster for me, old wise dudes!" I whine. Yes, I totally whine.

"If my theory—and I believe Hades and Persephone are on the same thought path as I am—is correct, your mother is the Goddess of Night herself." The king and queen nod grimly.

"Nyx?" Kyon sounds flabbergasted.

"The one and only," Charon snorts.

"So...how does that explain the memory and the shadows and...and me?!" I am getting so sick and tired of people talking around me, over me, above me, *about* me. Throw me a preposition and I'm done with it!

"Sweetie, what they are saying is that if Nyx is your mother, she would have been using the shadows to sneak around. Also, if you are the daughter of Nyx—which makes sense with your ability to shadow jump—the shadows can talk to you." Persephone hands me a snifter of amber fluid.

"Shadows...talk?" Could that be the talking I keep hearing in my head?

"From what I remember from Nyx, it isn't so much as talking. More like showing. That would explain why you have that memory." Lifting his drink from the arm of his chair, Hades swirls the amber drink around. "I'm not sure why she was hiding you away, though."

My world feels like it should be opening with the knowledge of who my mother most likely is, but it almost feels even more claustrophobic.

Needing to move to busy my hands, I stand from my place on Kyon's lap and walk over towards the bookshelves. I pull Tod from the sheath and spin him in tight clockwise movements against my palm. The light catches the silver and copper blade. As I peruse the shelf in front of me, I freeze, nearly dropping Tod.

Sheathing my destiny, I take the dark tome from the shelf. *Keeper of Night and Shadow* is scrawled in an elegant, silver calligraphy. It calls to me deep in my bones. When my fingers flip the cover open and touch the aged pages, something settles in me.

Chapter Thirty-Six

Kyon

S TYX'S EMOTIONS ARE ALL over the place as the ancient deities discuss Nyx's involvement and theorize why she would have hidden her baby Topside. I've been around nearly as long as they have been, but I don't know Nyx the way they do. Least of all as much as Charon.

"It would be safest for you to discuss this situation with her, my love," Persephone encourages.

Hades laughs, shakes his head. "No, no, my light. Nyx and I barely tolerate each other on the best of days. Charon would have better luck. He is favored."

We all turn to Charon; his complexion lightens a few shades as his mouth attempts to form words. His lips pop open and closed silently.

"Charon, please? I know you want what is best for Styx almost as much as I do. If you can help answer some of these questions..."

"Kyon, I can't. She will take that as me going against her. What's worse is if we're wrong." Charon shudders dramatically.

"She's your mother. Are you telling me that there is no possible way to ask her if Styx is your sister without incurring her wrath?" I ask, urging him to see a different aspect of the situation.

"Sister," Charon whispers as if tasting the word. "I hadn't thought about that implication." He sounds mystified at the prospect. Nyx has many children, so the idea of adding one more to the mix isn't unheard of. It's the abandonment of one that has everyone drinking brandy and discussing the probability of Nyx's ire unleashing unfathomable darkness onto the Underworld as we know it.

"What other option do we have?" I ask.

As they continue to bicker diplomatically, my gaze moves over to Styx. I watch her as she fidgets with her sword. Light reflects off the silver blade creating a unique show against the walls and ceiling.

Her mind is a jumbled mess, never settling on any one thought. Her emotions are even worse. Crackles akin to Zeus' lightning zip and collide against raging fires and thick, black clouds of depression.

Attempting to calm her mind along the bond, I push some calm towards her. I don't know if that's something I can do, but it won't hurt to try. I think of my greenhouse and all the plants and flowers I have nurtured to life. It is there I find my Zen, and I let it glide down the bond that ties us together, hoping it works.

Phantom whispers, soft and indecipherable, slither into my mind.

Then suddenly, she is sheathing her blade and picking an old, black tome from the shelf. The whispers grow in strength as if the source of them is getting closer. I peer at the title, seeing it clearly with my keen eyesight, *Keeper of Night and Shadow*. A book about Nyx?

Styx carefully smooths the pads of her fingers across one of the weathered pages and the whispers become more urgent. I've never heard whatever language they are speaking. At least, I don't believe I have. They are going so fast and there are multiple voices jumbling over one another, it's difficult to tell.

Putting both hands under the book so it lies flat across her palms, Styx whispers something causing the pages to flutter. She repeats herself and the pages whip to life as if an invisible hand is quickly flipping each sheet.

As quickly as it began, it stops.

"Thanks," Styx whispers.

"What was that?!"

"I found it." Her red eyes snap to my golden ones, glassy and ablaze with surety and magic?

"You found what, exactly?" I ask, sensing the others slowly moving closer to us from across the room. I wonder how much of that they witnessed.

"This ancient tome explains all of it...I think. It doesn't make sense, though. I mean...how can a book that looks older than Zeus possibly have the answers to what I am experiencing now? Me, of all demons!"

Even though she sounds like she is on the borderline of another anxiety attack, her emotions are as calm as the river from which she takes her name.

"I am no one. Another demon among droves. But this book clearly says, 'fuck all that noise, this is all about you, bitch.'"

"Little flower, you are not 'no one.' You are my mate. My heart's fire. Trust me, you are *not* just another demon."

"Show us what you found, Styx. Let us help you make sense of it all," Hades suggests calmly. His tone is one I've heard many times when he and I were training young Cerberi. The one that soothed the beast, allowing it to know it was safe.

"It's right here." She points to the open page with one hand while tilting the book towards Hades with the other. I don't miss her reluctance to let go of the tome.

"It's written in Koine Greek." Hades shakes his head slightly, then looks at Styx. "You can read it?"

She cocks a brow up. She's insulted, I can feel it. "Why, because I am a stripper and a grunt, I can't possibly know how to read?"

Straightening his spine, Hades says, "That is *not* what I was alluding to. Besides, you are no grunt." He reaches a hand toward the book, his pointer finger protruding from his fist. "This is a dead language. It isn't used anymore, let alone taught. A shame, really, it's absolutely beautiful to listen to."

Styx, stunned into silence, looks back down at the page,

"I mean...the whispers. Did you hear the whispers?"

"What whispers?" Charon asks as Hades shakes his head no.

"I heard them along the bond, my little flower. I couldn't understand what they were saying, though. The closer you got to the book, the louder they became. Especially when you touched the pages."

"Would you say you felt compelled to pick up that book?" Charon asks.

"Yes...and no. It was more like they were calling to me, pointing me in the right direction."

"The whispers?" Persephone probes.

"Yes. They kept telling me to look, to get closer. That this particular book had the answers I am looking for. And they were right."

"The Muses," Charon breathes out in fascination.

"The Muses? As in 'inspire me to write the next best-selling novel?' *Those* Muses?" Styx asks, mystified.

Charon nods before he begins pacing. Four steps away, four steps back. Repeat. "I would be willing to bet that it was Clio, the muse of history, attaching herself to you. The other voices are her sisters, working together to make sure you got the message."

"Yeah. I got it. Loud and fucking clear," Styx grumbles.

Chapter Thirty-Seven

Styx

"**Y**You should feel honored. The Muses don't choose just anyone to communicate with. Correct me if I'm wrong, Hades or Persephone, but I don't ever recall them choosing a demon before." Both king and queen shake their heads after a moment of thought.

"Great. Wonderful. Fucking marvelous! Not only am I supposed to break a metal prison, kill demons who are breaking all kinds of laws, but I am being targeted by the Muses??" Shit! Did I just say all that out loud?

No. You screamed it.

Shut the fuck up, you...

Dog got your tongue?

You aren't a part of my crazy, are you?

No, Styx. I am not.

Who the fuck are you, then?

Now isn't the time to get into that. I promise, we will talk about it, but you have enough to worry about at the present time.

"The Muses are not a negative force. They are goddesses who are meant to inspire and nurture. Most commonly, they are synonymous with artists and poets, but they are more than just that. As you witnessed, they help when a person...or a demon, apparently...are in great need," Persephone explains gently. She wraps an arm over my shoulders, offering support.

"Yeah? Then where were they when I was seven years old, huh? When I was starving, near death, and freezing my ass off? Or when I was eating out of garbage cans and breaking into cars to sleep in? Hiding from dark and evil men with greasy smiles and bad breath. No one whispered to me then, why now?" I don't care if I'm rambling, throwing all my low moments at their feet. I needed help then. I needed someone to care about me and give me a safe place *then*.

"I can't speak for the Muses, or for anyone else, for that matter. And I know you don't want my sympathy, but you are safe now. I will die a million deaths before I allow you to ever live like that again. You are mine, and I take care of what is mine. Even if what is mine knows how to take care of themselves." Kyon leans down and rubs his cheek against mine, a motion I've seen him do with both his best friend and his daughter. My heart melts and I feel my ire quieting.

"I feel sorry for anyone that attempts to harm either of you," Persephone quips with a quiet chuckle.

I suck in a deep, steadying breath, returning my focus to the book in my hand. Regardless of how I found the book, or why, I found what I need to move forward. I hope.

"A prophecy was written however many eons ago that seems to point right at me—if the Muses are to be believed. Listen to this:

The Child born of Shadow and Light
wielding a gift from Hephaestus' forge
will urge penalty for broken oaths
Three shall there be
To join her fight
First is the long-suffering Prisoner
Bound by soul and sword
Bringing with him experiences of war
Next is the Guardian
A pillar of courage and strength
Brandishing a goddess's blessing
Last is the Pure
Bearing the torch
To light the way of hope
and new beginnings

"I think there is more, but the next page is torn out," I explain after reading the prophecy.

Hades reaches for the book. "May I?" I reluctantly let him take it from my hands. The whispering that has been in the back of my mind this entire time fades away.

"I've never seen this book before," he says as he studies the cover with one finger holding the place of the prophecy. He opens it again, running his finger along the barely there edge of the missing page.

My fingers twitch with the need to have the book back in my hands. I feel incomplete.

Kyon slips his hand around mine, squeezing, grounding me. The heat of his body spreads across my back and my head drops back on his shoulder.

"The Guardian is obviously Kyon. He was blessed by Aphrodite's kiss when he was just a pup," Persephone explains. "The Prisoner...it must be whatever being is trapped in your sword. The Pure, though? I have no idea who that could be." Hades hands the book back to Styx who relaxes by degrees once it is back in her possession.

"I won't be fighting...whatever 'it' is by myself. That's a bonus." I try to play it cooler than I am feeling about this whole situation. I should be on a stage making money by shaking my tits at horndog humans, not deciphering ancient texts about some great destiny I'm meant to fulfill.

"There is something I don't understand...aside from the obvious. It says, 'child born to shadow and light,' but all of Nyx's children are born of darkness. Myself included." Charon lets that statement hang between us as the implications of it hits me full force.

"Y-you...I'm your..."

"If it's true that you are Nyx's daughter, yes. You are my sister," Charon admits uneasily.

Chapter Thirty-Eight

Kyon

HAT EXPLAINS WHY CHARON and Styx have a connection. Something inside of them must call to the other, like the connection I have with Ormr and my pups.

"Okay...so what's next? Do I just give Nyx a holler and say, 'Hi, Mom! Miss me?'" Styx, still clutching the book, pulls out of my embrace and plops into the nearest chair.

"I don't think that would go over so well. Besides, why would the prophecy call you 'of light?' *That* is the part I am stuck on. Nothing about Nyx is light." Charon sits in the chair across from my mate, Hades and Persephone take the two chairs to the left of Styx.

"It seems to me that your father may be someone other than Erebus." Hades shrugs his shoulders. It isn't unheard of for gods or goddesses to lay with someone other than their spouse. Zeus is the prime example of that.

"If we are looking for someone who would have left her with 'light' to Nyx's dark, who would we be looking at?" I ask.

"Well, as far as gods go...Apollo?"

"You're forgetting my sister, Hemera and brother, Aether. She is the personification of day, and he is the primordial god of light. Is it possible that Nyx and Erebus had a split kid?" I don't think he likes the idea that his mom stepped out on his dad.

"The only way we will ever know for sure is to talk to Nyx. We can theorize all night long, but it really won't get us any closer to knowing the truth. I'll talk to her. You know, gal to gal," Persephone says.

"It has to be me," Styx quietly utters. She looks around the room. "There is a reason she did what she did. I don't want more secondhand information. It's time I face my mother and ask her to be blunt with me."

"I'll go with you," I offer. My little flower looks at me, and for the first time since meeting her, I see love in her beautiful red eyes.

"I don't think you have a choice, Guardian." Smiling, she winks at me.

"All right, then. How do I summon the goddess of night?"

"It isn't as easy as knocking on a door, or even sending a messenger. Nyx is a very private woman. Besides, I would like to do some research first. If there is anyone in all the worlds I don't want to piss off—besides Persephone, of course—it's Nyx."

"Of course, Lord Hades. What should we do in the meantime?" I ask.

"I don't want to wait any longer, but I respect your determination and caution. I should probably return Topside, I'm sure Feather is worried," Styx concedes.

"I would love to show you around a little before you go," I admit, trying to keep the pleading out of my voice. If she goes Topside now, I don't know when I will be able to see her again.

Styx turns sorrowful eyes on me. *I won't be gone long, my guardian. You aren't getting rid of me that easily.*

"I can tell Feather what is going on...discreetly, of course." Without waiting for a reply, Charon bows to Hades and his bride before smoking out.

"Kyon, after you show her around and introduce her to your pups, you *can* go Topside with her. You are fated mates. I will not even entertain the idea of keeping you apart." With a loud clap of his hands, Hades decrees my freedom.

A peculiar thing, freedom. I've never once felt like a slave, trapped at times, yes, but never a slave. Yet, when the crack splits through the air, I feel as if I can breathe for the first time. I roll my head and notice the invisible collar is gone. The collars Hades gives us are mostly for our protection, especially when we are young and itching to get into mischief. And now, mine is gone.

Chapter Thirty-Nine

Styx

"Thank you, Lord Hades," Kyon says with a deep bow and a tear in his eye. "What just happened?"

"Hades blessed our union by granting me my freedom."

"What's more is that he is as free as you are to go Topside or come back to the Underworld whenever you want," Hades adds. Kyon and the God of the Underworld embrace. My mate rubs his cheek against the other man's face as Persephone places a hand on his shoulder. Kyon repeats the cheek rubbing thing with her.

"We will miss seeing you here all the time, but we are incredibly happy for you, Kyon."

"Tonight, we shall feast. I will invite your pups, if you'd like." Hades wraps an arm over his woman's shoulders and her face lights up.

"That is very kind of you, but I don't want to impose," I tell him, trying to not sound too excited about a dinner party. I have never been to one before, and it sounds exciting.

"You aren't imposing! The dinner is a celebration of your mating and for whichever of Kyon's pups he chooses, to be announced as his replacement. I believe you can use a little down time as well." Snapping his fingers brings the squat demon who answered the door for us.

"How may I be of service, Lord Hades?"

As Hades and Persephone make plans and do all that host stuff, Kyon pulls me off to the side of the library. "Little Flower, would you like to see my part of the Underworld?"

"A tour? I'd love that. I haven't seen much of the Underworld yet." Wandering around with Kyon might just be the distraction I need. My nerves are live wires, jumping and crackling. Honestly, I don't know what makes me more antsy; dealing with this whole destiny thing or meeting Kyon's family.

Have I become *that* girl? That is such a Nova thing to say, not me. Nope. I have lived my life not letting anyone in my bubble. If I needed to get my rocks off, I did so. No questions, no call-backs, no regrets. I didn't follow guys around hoping to meet their family. Yet here I am...itching to be completely immersed in Kyon's world.

It's the mating thing. Yup, that's it. All these mushy feelings are just residual magic. That's my story and I'm sticking to it.

"Want to shadow jump us there?" Kyon asks, pulling me from myself.

"Sure." Tapping my forehead, I say, "Want to show me where?"

Within moments we are standing in the shadows of a large...structure. Kyon shakes his head as if to clear it, his golden eyes blazing in the darkness. Gripping my hand tighter, he tugs me around the corner.

"I'm excited to show this to you." He opens a door and ushers me inside. I hear the click of the door right before the hum of lights coming to life. What greets me is far from what I could have ever imagined finding in the middle of the Underworld.

Three walls are ceiling to floor shelves, and each shelf is packed with flowers and plants. Colors, so many beautiful colors all over the place! Plants that should not be able to grow and thrive in Hell...the Underworld, whatever...are flourishing!

In the center of the space is a large hammock with a couple of pillows and a bright red blanket hanging off one side. It looks inviting after the long day I've had, but I am also curious about the plant life in here.

Kyon stands by the doorway as I inspect his private space. What I didn't notice at first glance are the books. As meticulously organized as the New York Public Library in Manhattan, his books line the bottom shelves around the room. Squatting, I run my fingers along their spines. All of them on this shelf are about botany, flowers and shit. The next shelf has books about human cultures.

"You like to read a lot, huh?"

"Whatever I can get my hands on. Charon brings me books from Topside when he can. Persephone does also." Kyon rubs the back of his neck sheepishly. "These are just some of my books."

"Let me guess, you've got a trove buried somewhere?" I tease.

The look of confusion on his face is quickly replaced by a smirk. "Smart-ass. Actually, I keep some of them in Hades' library where they are safer." Then he walks over to one of the shelves and pulls it like a swinging door. "Follow me." Not one to pass up exploring, I follow eagerly.

Rough stone steps that turn into the shadows beckon me. There is something precious at the bottom of these stairs, I can feel it. Kyon's excitement is flooding along the bond at whatever it is he has stored here. I sniff the air and only smell Kyon...and dirt of course. Am I the first person to come down here?

Just as we hit the landing at the bottom, that annoying tingle flares to life. "NO!" I bellow, startling Kyon.

"What's wrong, little flower?" he asks nervously.

"Oh, nothing...just this fucking destiny and ill-intentioned demons breaking laws at the most inopportune times." Noting the relief on his face that my outburst wasn't directed at him, I smile.

"I can go with you. Put a bit of Cerberi fear into the demon?"

"Let's go." I hold out my hand and the instant I have a firm grip, I jump through the shadows, allowing them to bring us where we need to be.

With Tod in my hand and Kyon at my back, I listen for the pull of the demon's exact location.

This way, little flower. Kyon keeps to the shadows, edging closer and closer to my mark. Then, as if a freak ice storm has run through him, Kyon freezes. Along the bond I feel his anger fighting to break free.

Only it isn't his anger that busts out into the night.

Chapter Forty

Kyon

W HEN WE STEPPED OUT of the shadows, I expected we would be Topside in some big city. Instead, we are somewhere in the Underworld I don't recognize.

Dipping my head back, I stick my nose into the hot air and inhale deeply. Something catches my attention, a scent that doesn't make sense. Or maybe I can't place it, I don't know, but whatever it is, I need to get there about five minutes ago.

This way, little flower, I send along the bond. Keeping to the shadows, I lead my mate towards whatever demon she is being sent to hunt down.

I round a corner of stalactites and freeze. The sight in front of me has my beast fighting to take over. I let him.

In a matter of seconds, my three headed form is leaping towards the demon before me. The demon who has the balls to be hurting one of *my* pups!

The scent, I realize now, is my pup scared and in pain.

Red washes over me as I swat the demon away with one burly paw.

"KYON! WAIT!" my mate screams for my attention. *We need to question the demon. This isn't normal. Hades will want him interrogated.*

MY PUP!

Kill him!

Destroy him! Both of my sides growl in my head.

NO! Tend to your pup. Leave the demon to me. Only for now, she reasons with all three of us as simply as breathing.

Forcing myself to turn my back on the demon and my mate, I belly crawl to my pup. She is hurt, but I can't tell how badly just yet. Even as her father, if I rush to her, she may fight back and hurt herself more.

Zephyra. It's your dad. The demon is gone. Come back to me, koutavi.

Daddy? Her mental voice oozes relief.

Yes. How bad is it?

I-I don't know. But I can't see anything. My eyes are swollen.

Where is that scum? Flower??

I have him. He's knocked out, but I am bringing him to Hades now. I'll be back in a couple minutes, our mate says, speaking as calmly as she possibly can. If she is able to hear my other personalities, I wonder if she can hear Zephyra, too.

Daddy, it hurts. She is already sounding weaker. Perhaps she will pass out and not have to feel this pain for a while. Depending on what the soon-to-be-dead demon used to hurt her, she should heal pretty quickly.

I shift back to my bi-ped form and scoop my daughter into my arms. Cradling her to my chest, I wait in the nearest pool of shadows for my mate to return. I close my eyes and wish that I could be in the protected home of Hades and Persephone instead of waiting.

The next thing I know, something tugs on me, and I am standing in the dark corner of the library in Hades' palace. My head whips around, looking for Styx, but she isn't here. What the fuck?

Little flower? Where are you?

Looking for you!

I'm in Hades' library.

What?

"How are you here?" she asks as she pops up next to me.

"I don't know. I wanted to be here and suddenly I was. I thought you came up behind me..."

"Cool. We'll deal with that later. Right now, Persephone is waiting for you upstairs," she informs me. Laying a hand on my shoulder, she jumps my daughter and I through the shadows with her. She opens a door and I find myself stepping into Zeph's room from her closet.

"Kyon, lay her down," Persephone commands.

Getting over the shell shock, I gently place my daughter on her bed. Now that I am able to see her injuries in the light, my heart breaks as a thunderous lividity tears through my mind and soul like a maelstrom.

Zeph's eyes are swollen shut and bruised. Blood is drying from her nose and mouth. Bruises color her body in a leopard pattern down her chest and abdomen. There are lacerations on her arms and chest. Her left knee is swollen three times its size, and her right foot is broken.

Three fingers from her left hand are missing, the blood is doing its best to clot. This is the area that Persephone tends to first by wrapping it up to stem the blood flow.

"It's going to be okay, Zephyra," I mumble, gently holding her uninjured hand. "We will make this right. I swear it."

"Daddy," Zeph croaks.

"Hush, koutavi. You need to rest. Persephone is here, you'll be okay."

I love you, Daddy.

"I love you, too, Zephy."

Chapter Forty-One

Styx

WATCHING KYON WITH HIS daughter, feeling his rage and panic, his fear and desire to dine on the demon who hurt her...it's all too much to bear. All of his feelings are as real as if they are my own.

On the other hand, I also feel like I don't belong here in this room. Warring with myself, I decide to check in with Hades and the demon down in the dungeon.

"I'll be right back." Unsure if any of them heard me, I skip through the shadows.

"Tell me who sent you." Hades' voice echoes against the stone walls and floors. His tone is one I haven't heard before, but the one I expected from him. Only worse. It has a scary undertone to it that could peel the skin off bones.

"No." The demon's reply is quickly followed by a grunt of pain. As I step closer, I can see why. Hades broke one of the demon's fingers. Seems like a small thing for the damage the piece of shit has done.

"Styx. Call for Malkiss," Hades commands calmly.

"On it." I'm excited to see Malkiss, it has been too long. And...to be honest, I want to see him work.

I jump through the shadows, allowing them to direct me to where Malkiss is at the moment. The more I focus on listening to the shadows, the more I hear them.

Instead of just telling me where to go, the shadows whisper to me, "Malkiss is sharpening his blades." Good to know. Thank you, Shadows.

"Knock knock," I say from the dark corner of his chambers.

"Styx? What in the hellfire are you doing here?"

"Nice to see you, too. Look...Hades needs you and your expertise. Come on. I'll explain later."

At the mention of the Lord of the Underworld, Malkiss takes the blades he had been sharpening and packs them in his 'doctor's kit.' The worn bag is magicked to hold a lot more than it should without anything clanging against anything else. Sort of like Hermione's bag in the Harry Potter books. (Yes, I'm a geek. Want to fight about it?)

"Shadows?" he asks.

"Shadows." He grips my hand and I whisk him away to the palace. Who knew this little trick would be this damn crucial?

"You're in for it now, demon sludge!" I hoot as Malkiss steps out of the shadows and to the table to set up his toys. Er...I mean, his tools.

"If you are going to stay to watch, I suggest you keep your mouth shut," Malkiss grunts. I know the drill, even if I have never been in the same room while he worked. The number one rule is to shut up and stay out of the way.

I mock zipping my lips closed and step back away from the light. Hades comes to stand beside me. He turns his head towards me and says quietly, "Thank you."

I nod and return to watching Malkiss with great interest.

Although it is a little cliché, Malkiss unveils his leather spanner roll. His tools, both sharp and purposely dull, catch the fire light from the torches. All the blades and pliers look brand new due to his meticulous care of each implement.

In his kit, he keeps wire cutters, pliers, a hammer, and a saw. All basic things that could be in any home improvement kit. He even has bamboo shoots and other seemingly innocent devices.

However, there are more sinister items in Malkiss' possession. Such as the Pear of Anguish. It looks like it could be a decorative something or other, but it is actually quite the opposite. The bulb of the pear is inserted into the victim, and then the torturer opens the pear, think of a sharp metal flower blossoming. It is not a pleasant thought at all!

I watch with wide eyes as Malkiss picks up the first tool. His fingers move deftly over the metal as if he's caressing a lover. I guess in some manner of speaking, he is.

Malkiss is a gentle soul, despite his looks and reputation. He has a strict code which depicts who he is willing to punish, and for what crimes. When he deems a situation worthy, he goes full throttle into his work.

This pathetic excuse for a demon, though? He crossed many lines with his crime. Not only was he torturing one of Persephone's Cerberi, but a female one at that! Malkiss has no tolerance for either of those crimes, therefore, he will take great pleasure in his work tonight.

"These are pliers. Most commonly used to twist wires or to help grip things, such as a pipe." Malkiss holds the pliers up in front of the demon's face, turning them this way and that. "Tonight, they will be used in a more unorthodox way." The calm manner in which he speaks is chilling. And I'm not even the one on the receiving end of it!

He takes the pliers and clamps them onto the horn jutting out from the left side of the demon's forehead. With his incredible strength, he snaps the horn in half.

The demon screeches in pain far worse than when Hades broke his finger. Interesting.

"Now, is there something you'd like to tell me, friend?" Malkiss asks.

Ichor oozes from the broken horn, it splashes on Malkiss when the demon shakes his head.

"Oh. Well, perhaps if we remove your other horn, you might decide to talk." Malkiss puts words to action, eliciting another screech. This one is higher pitched, and I think it's because the break is lower, closer to the skull.

"What about now? Any tales you'd like to share?"

This goes on for a long time. Malkiss has moved from the pliers, after pulling each claw out from the demon's fingers. The whole time speaking in dulcet tones, acting like he is trying to get a confession from a child.

A sharp crack as the hammer smashes the demon's collarbone has the demon gurgling in pain.

"Why were you hurting one of the Royal Cerberi?"

"In-infor...mation."

"For whom?"

"He wants...wants...intel."

Malkiss rotates his wrist, causing the hammer to arc around and catching the demon's focus. He taps the hammer on the demon's knee. Judging by the increase of sound, the hits are getting harder with each pass.

"ELIGOR!!!" The demon shouts.

Malkiss turns towards Hades, and I follow his gaze. Hades nods shallowly, giving Malkiss some sort of signal. Turning back to the demon, I watch as Malkiss knocks him out.

"Heal him and we will start again in a few hours," Hades states, obviously for my benefit.

"But he gave you a name. Why not just end it? Not that he deserves mercy by any means."

It's Malkiss who answers me. "Any name can be given under duress. We must research his claim. If it pans out, we will decide his fate then. If it doesn't..."

"Then you torture him anew to get the real information from him. Outstanding!"

"You have a thirsty heart for torture," Malkiss smiles. "Perhaps some day I shall teach you all my secrets."

"I thought you weren't my teacher, Mal," I tease, remembering the phrase he so often said to me before teaching me something.

He winks and moves back to his tools to clean them off. Then, and only then, will he begin healing the demon.

"Let's go check on Zephyra," Hades suggests, leading me out of the dungeons.

Chapter Forty-Two

Kyon

W ATCHING MY YOUNGEST PUP writhe in pain has my blood boiling. The only
thing keeping me from shifting and going to the dungeon to kill the demon
responsible is knowing that my mate is handling it.

Zephyra's brown hair is matted with blood and sweat, making it look muddier than
it normally is. I use the bowl of water and small towel that Persephone had waiting to
carefully wash Zeph's face and hair. She's finally passed out, but I don't want to risk
hurting her.

I move on to her neck where blood, sweat, and tears pooled while she was—I can't go
down that road. I can't think about how she got these injuries, or I won't be able to get
through this. Fuck, that sounds selfish. I want to stay here and tend to my pup, but every
time I think of what that poor excuse of a demon did to her...

Fuck it. Let's kill him.

Do it. We will feast on him for decades!

No. Hades needs answers.

Hades...he will let us kill him.

Hades loves us.

I will request it of him. And with that silent conversation, my calm has returned. At
least enough to focus on my pup. My koutavi.

As I clean her, Asclepius is working his healing magic. As the son of Apollo, he has been
given quite the gift, and training to go with it. That much is evident as he sets bones and
stitches muscle together again in the proper positions.

"It will be a few hours, at least, for Zephyra to fully heal the majority of her wounds.
This laceration here," he points to her thigh, "may take longer."

"Was it that deep?" I ask, concern lacing my words.

Asclepius, having a softer demeanor than his father, looks to me and smiles almost sadly. "I don't know how much you know or want to know about the manner of the attack."

"All of it. If you can tell me anything to help me understand why this happened...how I can help her better, I want to hear it. Please."

Styx chooses that moment to step into the room with Hades. "How is Zephyra?" She grips my hand tightly in hers as she sends comfort along our ever-strengthening bond.

"Asclepius is about to tell me. Please, continue."

"Judging by the order in which she received her wounds, this was an interrogation. Minor bruises and cuts first, that sort of thing."

Hades nods solemnly. "Yes, we just witnessed one of the best in interrogation skills work on Zephyra's attacker."

"Right. Most of her lacerations and breaks have been corrected...healed. The one that concerns me is the deep laceration on her thigh. It was made with copper. It will take longer to heal and may make it difficult for her to bear weight. Shifting might make it worse, so Zephyra will need to be monitored closely." Asclepius looks back at his patient. "She is made of strong stock, Kyon. She will get through this in one piece."

Persephone takes my other hand. I feel her strength next to me as warm as the firepits. "Will she be able to shift once she's healed?" she asks.

"There is a great chance that she will have her abilities back in a few weeks." Al answers

"But?" Styx questions. Her tone tips a bit higher.

Al sighs. "There is also a small chance that the leg will be weak for the rest of her life."

"Hades? Can't you pull out any copper that is still in there?" I implore him. He has an affinity for metal, it stands to reason that he will be able to pull it out of her system.

"It will be touchy. There is a great deal of iron in blood, and if I'm not careful..." he lets the implications hang in the air.

Releasing both Styx and Persephone's hands, I sit on my daughter's bedside. I brush my fingers over her forehead and down her temple. Her coloring has returned, and the bruising is gone. All that's left is rest and that damn copper. "Do it." Realizing I've just commanded my lord, I look up apologetically. "Please?"

Hades studies my eyes as he seems to think over whether he should make this attempt. I know of all the demons, gods, and goddesses, none—save Persephone—are more dedicated or protective of the Cerberi as a whole. Especially the pups. He would never do anything to intentionally hurt any of us.

"One condition," Hades states

"Anything."

"If I feel that I am doing more damage than good, I pull out. No arguments."

"Deal. No arguments. I trust you, Lord Hades."

Persephone quietly ushers everyone out of the room. Asclepius stays with Hades to help monitor Zephyra's blood iron levels, or something along those lines. It is hard leaving my pup's side, but I know Hades needs to concentrate.

"Kyon, why don't we go for a walk while Hades works. Persephone can call for us when Zephyra wakes up?" Styx asks, looking at the goddess for confirmation.

"Of course. Go, clear your mind. Zeph is safe here." Persephone hugs us both and sends us out the door.

I need...

We need to find that demon.

To protect our pup and our mate.

To blow off steam, I tell them. Their grunts of dissatisfaction have me shaking my head. One of us needs to be the cool and collected one. If I listened to them at all times, there would be a lot of decaying bodies in the Underworld. Righty would rather kill all the demons and start over while Lefty wants to hoard all of our most prized possessions and loved ones away from everything else. I have to be sensible. I have to keep them from going on killing sprees and benders. But they are me as much as I am them. I'm sure they have grievances with me as well.

"Where should we go? Should we tell your other pups what happened?" Styx wraps herself around one of my arms as if she was some damsel in distress. To the outside, that is exactly what they would see. However, I know she is only trying to comfort me in the only way she knows how. Contact.

"I don't want to alarm the siblings just yet. The girls are inside the palace, so they will be safe. The boys will want for blood, so it's best to wait until Zephyra is standing. Or at least sitting up." My boys are strong, intelligent, and capable of controlling their tempers...that is, until one of their siblings is in trouble. Hades will have my balls if the boys ransack the dungeons.

"I get that." Styx walks a few steps, still clutching my arm. Her breasts cocoon my bicep as her arms and hands circle my forearm. She isn't a small female by any means, but she is shorter than me by a few inches at least. Her body moves with mine as simply as if we were one. Her right leg moves at the same time as my left. Synchronicity at its finest.

Taking a breath, she says, "When I can't get my mind to settle, I dance. Not even on stage, just in my shabby apartment. Even if there is no music playing and people are standing all around, I'll dance." Rambling Styx is an adorable Styx.

"I go to my greenhouse and tend my plants."

"Let's do that then. You can dig in dirt, and I'll dance for them. Who knows...maybe you have some flowers that will bloom to the sway of my hips!" My little flower laughs as she sways said hips dramatically, pushing me to the side and back, nearly toppling me. Nearly.

Chapter Forty-Three

Styx

WE ENTER KYON'S GREENHOUSE shortly after. "You were taking me downstairs to show me something...?" My attempt is based partially on my curiosity, and partially on distracting him. More the distraction thing, though. He needs that more than I need answers. But unholy hell, I want to know what is down there!

"Right. Downstairs..."

"We don't have to go down there now. It can wait. Why don't you tell me about your favorite...plant?" I wave my arms out, indicating all the shelves heavy with greenery and all the colors of the rainbow. "Or how you got into doing all of this? I mean, to have plant life like this in the Underworld, that has to be some super unheard-of shit."

"Oh, well, Charon goes Topside a lot, of course. He had this scent on him once that I never experienced before. It was a plant called eucalyptus. It made me feel...right. As if all three of us were finally on the same page." He steps over to one of the bookshelves and squats. Returning to me with a book in his hands, he flips through the pages. "See?"

The open page shows me what the plant looks like and describes where it best thrives and all that geeky plant stuff. I try to show interest for his sake. Then something he said snags on me like a thorn. "The three of you?"

"Yeah. Lefty, Righty, and me. You heard them talking before, didn't you?"

Cocking my head to the side, I try to recall what he is talking about. "Who are they?"

"My other personalities. The other heads...you know, one on the left, the other on the right?" He seems to be confused by my reaction.

"OH! I thought that was just you talking over the issues to yourself. I do that a lot. Well, when I'm not talking to my other self. Actually, we've recently discovered it isn't a split of my personality rather than the voice of whoever is trapped in my sword." I glare at Tod. All this time I thought I was a little loony and he never told me the truth.

Explanations soon. I promise, my halo.

Yeah...and don't call me that.

He snickers at me, the bastard.

"Lefty...Righty. Are those their names? Seriously?"

Kyon raises a brow at me. "What else would I call them? They are still me. We are all Kyon."

"I don't know...maybe something a little more...fun?"

He smiles for the first time since just before we found his daughter. That enigmatic smile warms my heart and makes my pussy clench. Hot damn! "Fun? Like Balloons and...and...Trivia?"

I make an exaggerated disgusted face. "You obviously didn't name your children. Oh! Please tell me that you didn't name your sons after board games or something!"

There it is. Kyon's deep laughter bubbles out of him. "No." He shakes his head. "They have strong names. And yes, I did name all of my children, as is my right as their father."

Okay, so this all begs the questions about their mothers. If it is his right to name his offspring, what rights do the mothers have? I haven't heard anyone mention them, let alone seen any possible female Cerberi aside from his two daughters. Studying his face, I wonder how soon is too soon for me to be asking about his 'exes,' if you can even call them that.

"I can hear your thoughts, you know. You are horrible at masking them," he teases. "Most females are not maternal creatures. Especially those that are meant for breeding. Sure, they work as hard as the males and have the same duties and privileges, but bringing new life sets them apart from the males," Kyon explains easily.

"Not maternal? So, they don't care about the pups they bring into this world?"

"I wouldn't go so far as to say that." Kyon takes my hands in his and pulls me towards the hammock. Somehow, he manages to get both of us settled in the swinging net without toppling either of us onto the floor. "There are not as many females as there are males, therefore they are bred more often. This leads to dozens of pups in their lifetime. For example, I have thirteen pups with four different mothers. Those four mothers have also birthed pups for some other of the high ranking Cerberi." As he explains, he repositions us so that I am lying with my back to his chest, my head resting comfortably on both his shoulder and pillow. His large, warm hands casually rub up and down my arms in slow glides.

"Wow!" That's all I can think of to say. Wow.

"The females care about each of their pups to the point of not wanting them to be hurt, wanting them to be strong and powerful. However, they don't have the same kind of bond with them as the fathers tend to. I don't understand it, but it has worked that way for many millennia."

I listen with rapt attention as Kyon goes on about what the mothers of his pups are like. Part of me expects to be jealous, but he doesn't give the impression that any one of them meant anything more to him than that of an incubator. The humans would be appalled at the idea. I laugh to myself.

"You are amazing," he whispers into my hair. "From what I have read, non Cerberi females tend to be fiercely jealous of other females. Yet, you don't seem bothered at all."

"I thought you could read my thoughts?" I love teasing him.

"I was focused on what I was talking about. Why? What were you thinking?" He kisses my hair this time.

Turning my head so I can almost look into his eyes, I say, "You don't have a romantic feeling towards any of them. They were...a job, just like when I dance at the club. I don't care what any of those humans think of me. I am only in it for the money. It's the same thing."

Kyon growls at the mention of my dancing for the hornballs at the French Tickler. "How is that the same?" He tries desperately to not clench his jaw while he speaks. I kiss the side of his chin that I can reach, and he loosens up a bit.

"Well, as I said, I do it for the money. You do *it* to carry on your...genes, I guess. To have pups of your own to train and love. A legacy. Of course, that makes you sound less shallow than me, but let's face it, money talks, baby!" This earns me another laugh that vibrates through his chest and into my back. I love it!

"True. I guess I am just less materialistic than you."

Chapter Forty-Four

Kyon

FEELING HER BODY REACT to mine, even just the small touches along her arms make her shiver in the slightest way, and I am all for it! She is responsive. Yet, it is so much more than that. She wants to be touched, craves to be loved and cherished. My little flower will never admit it...out loud...but I hear her loud and clear. It doesn't even come from her thoughts, per se, but from her body. Her scent, the way she moves, and, most of all, her eyes. Those molten red eyes are so fucking expressive that I want to drown in their depths for all eternity. One flick of a gaze my way and all my troubles seem to just...fade away.

"I just like money. I like to gather it up and hoard it so no one else can touch it. Buy only the necessities and save the rest, that's my creed," she says with finality.

"When was the last time you bought something you didn't need?"

"Hmm. I...huh. I honestly don't remember."

"Clothes?"

"Only for work. Same for makeup, shoes, and underwear. My bras. Those I order for me, but they are still a necessity."

"I don't believe that. What about hobbies?"

She shrugs one shoulder against my chest. "I hunt. I dance. I sleep. And I fuck."

That's it? That's her life? "I don't like that," I growl.

"What? That I don't have a hobby?" Her tone is innocent, but she knows damned well what I was referring to.

"The fucking. Call me the jealous type if you must, but I don't want to hear about you fucking anyone but me." I roll and move her, so she is on her back and I am on my side looming over her.

"What if the others in the prophecy have huge cocks? Am I not allowed to play with them?" That damn smile tears into my heart.

"Did I collar you? No. Therefore, I do not control you." Although every fiber of my being wants to in the most primitive way possible.

We should collar her, Lefty growls excitedly.

We are all she shall ever need in life, Righty pipes in.

"I don't kno-ow," she sing songs. "Collaring could be pretty hot." My naughty little flower flicks her tongue out against my chin.

YES! All three of us scream in unison. Fuck yes!

Wrapping my hand around her throat, I lean down and trail my tongue along the column of her neck to her jawbone. She lifts her chin to give me better access and I do it again. I take her cues to give her the sensations she wants all while making her guess if and when I will strike with my tongue. Or my teeth.

I tighten my grip around her throat, pressing my fingers into her flesh. She sucks in a breath, grabbing at my arm with her free hand, the other trapped between us. As I continue to lick, bite, and suckle on every part of her I can reach, she digs her nails into my skin.

I squeeze her throat a little tighter.

She tries to gasp for air, her eyes popping open and glaring at me. Not with anger, though, with raw desire. Her eyes practically screaming at me to fuck her and fuck her hard.

Who am I to ignore such a plea from my mate?

I release her throat, allow my nails to grow out into claws, and rip her shirt down the middle.

"Asshole! I loved that shirt!" she pants out.

"I'll get you a new one. Better say goodbye to your pants, too."

"No fucking way!" She pushes my hand away and pulls down the zipper at her hip. Miraculously, she is able to push the tight leather pants over her hips and down her legs with ease.

I see a flash of bright red go with the pants and I look down to see her neatly kempt pussy is bare to me. All she wears now is the matching red bra. And a smile. Gathering that she has a deep obsession with her bras, I choose not to slice and dice it. Instead, I carefully unhook the little bastards between her heavy tits. Once the clasps are open, her tits push the material as they fall to the sides slightly. I lean down towards the breast closest to me and nuzzle it with my nose, taking in the warm scent of her skin.

Wrapping my tongue around her pert nipple, I groan as she pushes her chest into my face. I let the tips of my claws trace along her ribs to her hip bone, then back up to her neglected breast. Pinching her other nipple, rolling it between my fingers, drags a distinctive purr from my sweet little flower.

"I'm all for nipple play, big boy, but this bitch needs your mouth elsewhere." Her voice is pure unadulterated sex. Husky and demanding. Needy and urgent.

Trailing my claws down to the apex of her thighs, I tap one of them against her damp curls. "Is this where you want my mouth? Do you want me to taste you? To drown in the sweetness that gathers there just for me?" Slipping my finger between her folds and teasing her clit, I watch as her pupils explode.

"Fucking goddesses, YES!"

Careful to not tip the hammock, I swing my right leg up and over her, placing my foot on the ground. In this position, I am lying on top of her, supporting my weight on one foot. As seamlessly as possible, I get my other foot on the ground, and pull myself up so that I am standing over her. "Pull your knees to your chest," I instruct her. It takes a moment, but her feet clear my crotch. I grab her ankles and lift them, so her legs are now straight in the air. My hands slide down the backs of her calves as I sit/squat, hooking her knees over my shoulders. I can already smell her arousal, the scent only getting stronger the closer my face comes to her pussy.

Slipping my feet out from under me so that I am on my knees, I dive nose first into the moist folds of my mate's core. Inhaling as I move upwards towards her hood, I curse myself for not taking off these blasted jeans first. The material is chafing my dick!

*Cerberus up! **Taste her!** Righty bellows.*

Coat our tongue with her juices. Don't let a single drop go to waste, Lefty urges.

You don't have to tell me twice...thrice? Fuck it! Shut up!

Taking all the advice, I open my mouth over her pussy and suck.

"OH FUCK!" she screams.

My tongue twirls and laps at all of her. It spears inside of her like a sword to a sheath. Licks at the velvety softness.

With her nails digging in my forearms, the noise that comes from her chest and throat would make any Cerberi proud. "Unholy fuck! I'm so...so...FUUUCKK!!"

As she comes, I fix my mouth over her and slurp up every. Last. Fucking. Drop. The taste of her is grander than anything I've ever enjoyed in my long lifetime. The nectar of the gods has nothing on the nectar of my little flower.

Chapter Forty-Five

Styx

K YON TOYS WITH MY clit, swirling and flicking his tongue against it. I have never had anyone make me come so much using only their mouth. My head is spinning, my body is quaking, and I feel as if I'm about to pass out. My face tingles and I tap his shoulder. "Persephone's Pomegranates! I need to breathe!" My throat is dry as I suck in as much oxygen as possible.

Panting, I look at his tousled brown hair, watching as he lifts his head and rests his chin on my pubic bone. His lips are glistening, swollen, and my pussy clenches. Kyon licks his lips, and his pupils expand impossibly wider, leaving the thinnest ring of fire around the black orbs.

With my breathing coming at a more normal pace, I tunnel my fingers into his hair. Gripping the strands, I tug in an attempt to direct him to bring his face closer to mine. Good puppy listens well, and soon I am tasting myself on his lips and tongue.

He pulls back and flicks his tongue across my lips. "I knew tasting you would be one of the greatest pleasures in both the Underworld and Topside. Though, I didn't expect it would be the best." I give him a crooked smile.

Kyon twirls a lock of my hair around his finger. His attention is fully on the dark strands as they ravel and unravel around the digit. I try to use the bond to look into his mind because he is obvious thinking pretty fucking hard. His eyebrows arrow down, forehead wrinkled, and he has his bottom lip trapped between his teeth. It's quite an adorable expression, especially for someone who can shift into a Cerberus at the drop of a claw.

He may be ancient and well read, but he is also innocent in many ways. He only knows the written word of Topside, and the things he has gleamed from Charon and Persephone. Judging by the relationships—or the lack thereof—he has had with the mothers of his pups, it is safe to assume that this whole mating thing is beyond his expertise as well. Not that I'm a scholar by any stretch of the imagination. There is so much he has to learn about me, my world, and life. On the same side of the token, I have much to learn about him. Both as a man and a beast.

Being considerate of another's feelings isn't my strong suit. Hell, cuddling after any kind of sexual experience is outside of my wheelhouse. I'm worried about his daughter, of course I've always been one to protect the female species above all others. But this is more than that. I want to protect Kyon. I want to make sure his pups are safe.

Not only do I find myself caring about Kyon, but I *need* him. I never would have imagined that I would ever tie myself to one man—in the non-kinky rope play way—yet, thinking about stepping back on Topside soil without him makes my heart hurt. Thinking of sleeping in an empty bed leaves me feeling bereft. Kyon opened my heart. He has helped me to see beyond myself.

"Kyon?" I murmur.

"Hmm?"

"Is my hair that interesting?" I smile when he looks up at me with wide eyes. "Whatcha thinking about?"

He drops my hair and exhales a sigh. "I'm sorry."

I wait for him to elaborate—see? Trying not to push him. Patience, my name is Styx. But my heart picks up its pace as a world of scenarios race through my overactive imagination. He realizes this was all a mistake. I'm not the one for him. I'm too mouthy and I have too much baggage. He doesn't want to spend the rest of his incredibly long life with someone as fucked up as I am.

Fuck me! I'm turning into one of *those* girls!

Finally, he begins to speak, and I steel myself for whatever 'it's not you, it's me speech' he has come up with. "This was amazing, and I ruined the mood. I'm sorry. I just...my pup is in pain, and I just snuck off to feast on my mate. I'm a horrible father."

Relief! But, aww!

"Kyon." I cup his jaw in my hands and urge him to look me in the eyes. "You are not a horrible father. Not by a long shot. You needed to take a break; Zephyra wouldn't fault you for that." His eyes are moist with emotion. "And...Persephone told you to clear your head, so there was no sneaking off."

"Nothing has ever distracted me from my pups before. Nothing could have made me leave that palace with one of them injured like that. Hades would have had to literally command me to take a step back. Yet...even though I am worried about my daughter, I walked off with you without a fight." Kyon is at war with himself.

"What do your other halves...thirds?...think about how you handled yourself?"

He tilts his head to the side as he confers with the other two parts of him. He has a better handle at blocking his mind than I do. "Neither of them regret any time spent with you. It settled their nerves, mine too, honestly."

"Then there you go. Would you like to go check on Zephyra now?" Look at me go...totally want to fuck his brains out, but I am putting him and his family first. Once upon a time, I would have gotten my jollies and sent the man on his way. Now, I'm cuddling, having conversations, and letting him know that I don't mind waiting for him. What in Zeus' testicles have the Fates done to me?

"This shirt looks like a damn muumuu on me," I grouse. "You can't see my curves! What the hell good is it to have a body if I'm not showing it off twenty-four-seven?" Secretly, I am loving the feeling of the worn-soft material against my skin. Not to mention the fact that it smells of my Cerberus.

"I may not be able to see your curves as well, but, my little flower, there is nothing sexier than seeing you in my clothes." Kyon pulls me closer and kisses me deeply. "Not only is my scent literally wrapped around your body, but everyone will know that I gave you at least half a dozen orgasms."

Ooh, my Cerberus is naughty, and it is hot as fuck! "That seals the deal for me! Let's go." I press up against his body and step back into the shadows. Within moments, we are stepping into the pools of light in the library. Persephone doesn't seem surprised by our sudden appearance. She must have been able to sense us coming into her domain again.

Chapter Forty-Six

Kyon

Persephone's lips quiver as they try to hide a knowing smile. Her eyes, although strained with concern, have a small twinkle in them. "Feeling more...in control?"

I lick my lips, tasting my little flower there still, and nod. "How's Zephyra?"

"I haven't heard anything yet. But it shouldn't be much longer. Are you hungry? Thirsty?"

While we try to ignore the passing seconds that seem like hours, we sit in a companionable silence. My mind is reeling with the possibilities of what could be happening in the room upstairs.

The sound of a door creaking and then heavy footfalls alerts me that Hades is now leaving Zephy's room. From the shuffling, I am willing to bet that Asclepius is helping the weakened god, which proves how much Hades trusts the God of Healing. Persephone tells us we can go upstairs and sit with Zephy, and Asclepius will be in with us soon. Then she rushes up the stairs to her mate.

"Do you want me to wait for you down here?" Styx asks.

I take her hand without a word and lead her up the stairs. Opening the door, I'm pleased to see Zeph's eyes open...a bit glossy, but open.

"Daddy," she croaks, wincing as if talking hurts her throat.

"Shh, I'm here." I tap my head, encouraging her to use our bond to speak.

Who is she?

"Zephyra, this is Styx. My mate." My daughter's eyes widen as she claps her hand over her mouth. I know she wants to scream; I can literally hear it in my head. Smiling, I officially introduce my little flower to my youngest pup. "See if you can hear Zeph, little flower."

Testing, testing. Can you hear me, Styx? Zeph projects, hopefully to both of us.

"I can." My little flower's eyes are glowing. "I'm sorry we are meeting under such shitty circumstances."

From what Hades said, you saved my life. Thank you!

Fuck, I didn't even stop to think of that! She truly did. Had she not been alerted to the danger...or if she hadn't been able to shadow jump...

Daddy! Stop! I'm okay now.

"It's no big deal...I mean, it *is* because this is your life we're talking about...but I only did what I had to." Who knew my mate was the humble type? I love listening to her babble on, though. She doesn't take compliments well, it seems.

"Are you kidding? You deserve a national holiday for what you did. Little flower, you truly saved my heart in more ways than one." I lift our clasped hands to my lips and kiss her knuckles. The blush that creeps up her neck and cheeks melts me.

"I'll accept the gratitude, but not anything else. There really is no need for it. You both would have done the same thing if you were in my shoes. So, let's just drop it, yeah?" Nope, my girl has no desire to be in the limelight, which is quite ironic considering what she does for money. I shrug that off for now as all three of my personalities growl in unison.

"Consider it dropped. Zeph?" She nods in agreement.

"Can you tell us what happened? I mean, if it isn't too...difficult or traumatic. Malkiss did some interrogations, but he wasn't as successful as we'd hoped." I'd forgotten Styx was present for that.

I don't remember how I ended up with him, that's all a blur. But he kept asking me questions about security schedules and Persephone. Having been trained by both Hades and my father, I knew not to give him anything vital. Of course, he didn't like that too much and was wailing on me. I couldn't defend myself, couldn't shift. I couldn't even call out for help mentally. I was cut off from everything.

"What kind of questions?" I ask, digging my nails into the palm of my free hand.

Odd ones. He asked if she and Hades slept in the same room, if they dined together. I denied knowing anything about their private life. Then he kept asking about if there was ever a time Persephone wasn't being guarded. He also asked about secret passageways out of the palace.

"You didn't give him anything. Good job, Zephyra," I praise her, the worried father steps aside as the teacher takes center stage. "You kept to your training. I'm proud of you."

"He would ask questions about food and sleeping if he was trying to throw you off. Sort of like he was testing you and your loyalties. When you denied knowing, what happened?"

He punched me. As if he knew the answers and knew I was lying.

"Hmm."

"What is it, little flower?"

"Obviously, she doesn't know this demon, nor do you. That would have come up already. If he knows anything about what happens inside this palace, he has a contact on the inside."

You mean...there is a traitor *inside the palace?!* Zeph asks incredulously, and Styx nods.

"Fuck! We need to speak with Hades and Persephone. Now."

"Any idea of who it could be?" Styx asks.

There are at least two dozen demons, my sisters, and myself that are in and out of the palace on a regular basis. We all work here to some degree or another.

"We can rule out your sisters, they'd never put Persephone in danger. Or you," I state. My minds are pulling up scent files and images of each of the demons I am aware of that work in the palace. There are a few that I feel *could* be capable of treachery, but if they can fool Hades...they can most definitely fool me.

"That's a given. Another Cerberi would not need to torture one of their own for information they already have. Least of all one of their siblings. This reeks of a demon, for sure."

Chapter Forty-Seven

Styx

W HILE KYON LISTENS TO Asclepius about Zeph's injuries and what Hades was able to accomplish, I pop down to the rooms Malkiss is occupying.

"You want me to interrogate the entire demon staff?" Malkiss grunts. "I don't think Hades will want all of his minions—"

"Malkiss, please! Listen to what I'm saying to you. Your name strikes fear into the heart of most demons. Especially if they appreciate their positions they've worked for. Are you picking up what I'm laying down here?" The demon is exasperating!

Understanding loosens his jaw that he'd been clenching for the past half hour. "All I have to do is loom over them a bit. Not use my physical tools, but my mental ones. It could work, and Hades won't have to heal his staff." He seems to be talking to himself more than to me. "Fine. If Hades approves it, I'm in."

Finally!

I bring him to the palace, to the library, of course, and wait for the others to join us. *Kyon, Malkiss and I are here. Is Hades up for a chat?*

Yeah, he heals quite quickly. Be there in a minute, my mate assures me. My mate. I giggle to myself; I'm so not used to that.

"On their way," I tell Malkiss as he stands with his hands behind his back. He looks like an army general. This is the pose that says he isn't entirely comfortable. Malkiss is used to being in the dungeons or his own territory. Take him out of either and he behaves uncharacteristically.

"Malkiss, are you ready for round two?" Hades asks as he enters the library with Persephone on his arm. Kyon walks behind them both until he is able to move around them to get to me.

"Actually, Lord Hades, Lady Persephone, Styx requested that we meet together. Take it away."

"I had a thought. But first, is there any way to...I don't know...soundproof this room?"

Persephone nods, snaps her fingers, and suddenly all the noise from elsewhere in the palace is gone.

"Cool trick! Okay, so Kyon and I were talking to Zephyra, and we believe that the demon who attacked her was quite possibly working for someone inside the palace."

Persephone gasps and Hades' dark features grow darker. His eyes blaze with hellfire. "Elaborate," the god commands.

I give a detailed account of the conversation with Zephyra, and then the one I had with Malkiss. Everyone listens quietly and when I finish, we all look to Hades.

"I think that will be the best course of action. Kyon, you should shift in the dungeon and stay with Malkiss. Between the two of you—"Nope. I have to stop this shit right here. God or not. "Sorry, Lord Hades, but not only was this my idea, but I believe that I have a skill or two that will help."

Hades looks at me, tilts his head to the side, and glares at me. I glare right back.

I can feel Kyon's nervousness lashing me with whip cracks. *What are you doing!? Lower your eyes!*

Not going to happen. I'm from Topside, Hades does not have dominion over me.

You are in his home!

Kyon, I'm not afraid of him.

Oh, fucking Fates! What the hell kind of storm did you thrust me into!? I can't help but smirk at his theatrics.

"Join them," Hades states. "You are a ballsy one, aren't you?"

"You're just figuring that out?" I smile, still not blinking. I will not look away first.

Hades throws his head back and laughs, effectively looking away first. Win!

I can't...how did...what just??? Kyon is at a loss for words. When I look at him, his mouth is wide open, his eyes practically bulge out of their sockets, and he is as pale as a soul.

Sorry, mate. I'm not going to bow to anyone. Not you, not a god, and definitely not to any demon. I purse my lips together in a kiss and suck in as I let them pop open.

"What gifts do you possess that you believe will help with the interrogation?" Hades asks once he's calmed his laughter.

"For starters, Tod." I pull the sword out and buff it against the bottom of Kyon's shirt that I'm still wearing. "He senses demons who are breaking laws. That's how I found Zephyra, well, that and Kyon's noses."

"Wouldn't your sword be able to pinpoint the demon we are searching for rather than relying on Malkiss' reputation?" Persephone questions. Anyone else, I would have taken that as an insult, but she seems utterly fascinated and curious.

"Yes and no. The demon would have to be literally performing the unlawful deed. I'm not entirely sure how it works, but Tod can sense the nefarious behavior." I shrug, slipping Tod back into his sheath.

"Let's try it. I'll have each of the servants join you all in the dungeon. Good luck."

The three of us go to the oversized dungeon and 'set up shop.' When Hades suggested Kyon to shift, I didn't think his Cerberus form would fit down here. Apparently, there is an area of the dungeon that is dug deeper than the rest, allowing room for a full-grown Cerberus to stand comfortably. Who knew?

Kyon strips himself of his clothes and crouches down on all fours. His shift lasts all of fifteen seconds. As if I'm seeing him for the first time, I smile like a damn fool as he stretches and shakes.

"You are magnificent," I coo.

All three heads lower towards me. The one on the left, named Righty, carefully licks my cheek with the very tip of his tongue. The one named Lefty nuzzles me the slightest bit as Kyon's center head brushes against my back. I think he is trying to hold me up. Freaking adorable.

My heart. That isn't Kyon, that is one of the other heads.

My soul. Oh! This one has a different voice too. How wondrous!

"Lefty, Righty...you both need better names." I kiss each of their noses. "I'll find them as soon as possible. Promise."

Chapter Forty-Eight

Kyon

WATCHING STYX TREAT LEFTY and Righty with affection makes our hearts melt. She truly is a magnificent being. Promising to give them proper names just puts me over the top.

Malkiss looks on in what I can only describe as fascination as my real-life Beauty and the Beast interact with each other. "Okay you two. How do you want to play this?"

Turning around, Styx leans against one of my paws as my heads lift up to pay attention. "Well, we can have them come in, watch for tells. If that doesn't work, we can question them. Have you ever heard the phrase 'good cop, bad cop?'"

"Can't say I have."

"The idea is that one is more on the gentle side and the other more aggressive. We can implement a version of that. Let me do the talking, you and Kyon act as the muscle. Be intimidating and watchful," she explains easily.

"Works for me. Kyon?" Malkiss tilts his head back to look at me, and Lefty, Righty, and I all nod.

"Send in the demons!"

The plan is that they are all waiting by the north entrance and will leave through the east so as not to be able to discuss what happens in this area. We don't want them preparing the others. The first demon enters into our little headquarters. He has a cocky expression on his face when he sees Styx, but as soon as his beady eyes land on Malkiss and then me, he drops the tough guy persona.

"What is your name, demon?" Styx asks bluntly.

"Elios."

Truth.

"What is your job in the palace?"

"I work in the kitchens."

Truth.

"How do you feel you are treated by Hades and Persephone?"

"They are both pleasant. Although I am a servant, I am not treated as a slave. Not like some of the other deities do."

Truth.

"Do you wish them harm?"

"Never!"

Truth.

"Thank you, Elios. You may go back to whatever you were doing." The demon bows to her then squeezes against the wall—trying to keep as far away from me as possible—and slips out of the east door.

One by one, demons step up to Styx and answer the same questions. All of them, so far, speak the truth from what I can sense. Even the judgmental Lefty agrees. He is of the mind that all demons—with the exception of our mate—are prone to lie.

Fifteen demons later, Styx adds more questions to her list. I realize why moments later.

"When was the last time you left the Underworld?" she asks, seemingly out of left field.

"Oh. Ummm...I would say it has to be about ten Hallowed Eves ago. Some teenagers were attempting to summon some legend or another and I thought I would have some fun."

Something about that is a lie, I warn her.

"Hmm. A seance of sorts?"

"Y-yes."

"What were they using?"

"I-it was a umm, candle. A black one."

"Just one?" At the demon's nod, she continues, "That is very interesting, Satter. I thought to garner a demon's attention, they had to use thirteen candles."

"Oh, they had other candles. But only one black one."

He is lying.

I know.

"Who sent you?"

"W-what are you talking about?" His eyes shift quickly between me and Malkiss, then back to Styx.

"Who sent you?"

"It was, umm...I was granted the, umm...pardon for the hallowed moon."

"Who. Sent. You?"

"No one! I-I—" The demon's eyes roll to the back of his head and he falls to the ground headfirst.

"What the fuck?" Malkiss growls.

"Scared him. He is lying about the seance, but he isn't our traitor," Styx announces.

Agreed. I nod my heads for Malkiss' sake.

"I believe you are right. Let's make sure to tell Hades about that. We may need to look into this one some more." Malkiss picks up the demon and brings him to a small cell out of sight. Each cell was magicked to block sound for our purposes.

We are nearing the end of the staff, if my count is correct. Styx is getting antsy; I can feel it pulsing off her in waves.

"Next!"

Demons come in, they answer her questions, they leave. Not a single one has lied about a damn thing since the one in the cell behind me. None of them look guilty, just scared. Rightfully so.

"How many more demons are behind you?" Styx asks the slender, bird-beaked demon in front of her.

"I'm the last one."

"What is your name?"

"Karsha."

"Your job here in the palace?"

"I tend to the cleaning. One of the seven that do, of course. The palace is too big to do it all by myself. Although I could!"

"Do you have any enemies?"

"Not personally. That I know of. Well, no. That's not true. Feesha doesn't like me very much. But that's because I took her job. She didn't know how to fold laundry without slicing it with her claws."

"Anyone that would want to see you removed from Hades' employ?"

"Nope. I don't think so." She shrugs her pointy shoulders.

"Thank you."

As the last demon leaves through the east door, Styx comes over and sits on my paw. "I don't get it. I was sure the traitor was one of the staff."

Malkiss drops into a squat in front of my little flower. "Don't be too hard on yourself, grasshopper," Malkiss says with a grin. "When working with demons, it can be very difficult to find their tells. Especially because every single demon that walked through here looks different than the one before it."

"I know, but if one of them would have lied, Tod would have known. He only barely vibrated when that one was lying." Styx throws her head back with a frustrated growl. "This is bullshit!"

Little Flower, it isn't just Tod. I didn't sense anything notable.

"What about you, Malkiss? Did you pick up on anything?"

"No, I didn't. Just the natural fear of being so close to me and the Cerberus. Perhaps we are thinking too close to home, so to speak. Maybe there was someone who is no longer employed? Or a visitor that no one is thinking about."

"I need to figure this out before another Cerberi is hurt." My little flower is in protective mode, that's for sure.

We decide to meet back up later, come up with another plan after Malkiss and Hades interrogate the demon who attacked my daughter. Styx needs rest, to clear her mind.

Chapter Forty-Nine

Styx

"I AM PISSED, KYON! I have gone up against demons who think they have the upper hand. Demons violating humans for their own purposes. I've killed them with barely a thought." I pull Tod from my back and toss him onto an empty shelf in Kyon's greenhouse. "You did not help at all! After I had a stare down with the fucking God of the fucking Underworld to get my ass into the thick of things. I convinced him that you would help us. You piece of shit destiny! You suck!"

Livid. I am fucking livid! "All the nights when I had to go running out every time my head hit my pillow. All the miles I've raced through the city to slice and dice some mother fucker. All the fucking blood that damn sword gobbled up! And you couldn't help me this one damned time?"

My little halo, you have to understand that none of those demons are the one you are looking for. I would have known. I am not choosing to not be helpful.

"Don't you fucking call me that!"

"Flower? Are you okay?" Kyon asks.

"I'm fine. Just fucking dandy! This sword is pissing me off."

Kyon steps up to me, wraps his arms around my waist. "My little flower, come, rest."

Sighing, I droop against his chest. I know he's right. And so is Tod, even if I don't want to admit it. I'm just so frustrated with the whole situation.

"I'll give you a massage, how's that sound?"

Moaning deep in my throat, I drop my head back against him. "That sounds delish."

Kyon scoops me up into his arms and carries me across the room and through the hidden door. He carefully scales the stone steps into an area I have yet to see. With a magic I hadn't known he possessed, he literally breathes a little hellfire, lighting a torch.

"That was fucking cool! I didn't know you could do that."

"I don't do it often. Burns the throat a little," he explains with a small smile. "This will be more comfortable than the hammock."

Looking around, I am awed. Center stage of the room is a large—and I mean Large with a capital 'L'—bed. The sheets and blankets are neatly folded and tucked where they should be, making it look like something from a catalogue. There is a small fridge in the corner next to a sink and an oven. On the other side of the bed, there is what looks like a hot tub.

"This looks very cozy. And efficient."

"You like?"

"I love!"

Kyon kisses the top of my head and carries me to the bed. He strips me of my shoes and leather pants—carefully so as to not tear them—before lifting his shirt over my head and outstretched arms. "Lay on your belly. I'll be right back."

I do as he instructs, crossing my arms and laying my head on them. Watching as he moves across the room and digs around in a medicine cabinet looking for something, I can't help but smile. He is a delicious man. Protective, loving, intelligent, and patient. Above all, he is mine.

When he returns to the bed, he waggles a bottle of massage oil at me. "It warms as it is used, helping to relax the muscles."

The bed dips and jostles as he walks on his knees from the edge of the bed to the center where I am. He sidles up to me and puts one leg over me so that he is practically sitting on my ass. The oil squirts into his hand with a wet squeak. His calloused hands rub together, making a soft rasping noise until the oil is spread enough to silence the movement. Then his warm hands are on my shoulders.

His thumbs press into the tight muscles there, moving in small circles with just the perfect amount of pressure. I've only had one massage in my life, and it was nothing like this, and he's barely started!

As his hands work their magic, I lose track of what he is doing. If anyone were to ask me what all he did during this massage, I would not be able to answer. My eyes drift closed as a familiar soft hum serenades me into a light doze.

"Little flower?" His husky voice is right by my ear, pulling me from whatever zone I slipped into. "How are you feeling?" he asks when I moan happily.

"I'm great." It's then that I feel his hard cock poking into my side, and I realize he is lying next to me now. I turn my head, flipping my hair over so I can look at him. His eyes are alive, golden and bright, and burning with desire. "I need you to fuck me now, Kyon," I demand with a purr.

Kyon leans in and kisses my elbow, his hand now massaging my ass. "I love how juicy your ass is. All of you is perfect. Not like the skeletal humans I've seen in magazines." A light blush colors his cheeks and I feel apprehension from him. I think he is worried that he offended me.

"Baby, I love my curves. It's a good thing you do too, because I won't be going on some diet to become a beanpole for anyone."

"Thank Hades for that!" Kyon rolls me onto my back and immediately shoves his face into my neck. His knee pushes my legs apart. He kisses and licks at my neck as his hard cock pokes into my thigh.

"Bite me, Kyon. Claim me and mark me as yours," I demand of him.

With a thick, pleasurable growl that vibrates through me, he snags the spot between my neck and shoulder with his teeth. He teases me, nibbling, barely biting down. One hand is tangled in my hair, holding my head to the side and out of the way.

"BITE ME!" I growl out loudly between my teeth.

And he does.

And it is glorious.

A heaviness builds in my abdomen, my pussy clenches, and he continues to bite. Not hard enough to do major damage, only enough to make me bleed.

Your blood is the second best flavor of you, he says in my mind as he runs his tongue over the bite mark between his lips. I feel his throat working as he swallows. And swallows.

I come, gripping his arms, his sides, I don't know...could be his foot for all I know. Pleasure. Pure, unadulterated pleasure pulses through me as I ride out my orgasm with my mate latched to my neck.

Once it subsides and I can breathe a bit better, Kyon lines his monstrous cock up with my pussy. I'm not as concerned with the size of it as I was the first time, knowing I can take him despite how large he is. He eases in slowly and I can't take it. I need fast, hard, and aggressive fucking!

I wrap my legs around his waist, hooking my feet behind him. "For the love of Persephone! FUCK ME!" I snap my hips up, using my heels to pull him into me. We both groan as his full length settles into my pussy. "Oh, fuck!"

"Did I hurt you?" he asks, genuinely concerned.

"No!" I pant out. "You call me a little flower, for some unknown reason, but I am not delicate. Fuck me, Kyon."

And he does. Hard. Fast. Deep.

Within moments, I am coming again. And again. I relish in every rib of his penis, each spiraled bit of him. The pattern touching the walls of my vagina at different times and different pressures rocks my fucking world in a way I never could have imagined. My head spins with the sensations he is giving me as he pushes in and pulls out.

You pulled in my knot...

Sweet! That's all I can think of to say. I don't give a rat's ass at this point. I am lost in the feel of him. The absolute pleasure he gives me.

"I am going to come in your hot pussy. Fuck!" His cum shoots into me, warming me more than I thought possible after all the friction. And I orgasm right along with him.

The knot he told me about is swollen just inside my pussy. It throbs as my muscles clench around him.

Kyon wraps his arms around me and rolls over to his back, pulling me so that I am lying on top of him. "Just relax. The knot will settle soon," he says as he rubs my back some more. The pressure is lighter, more like he is drawing pictures on my skin, and I feel even more relaxed than before. A great orgasm, or five, will do that to a gal.

"Tell me something about you...I don't want to fall asleep yet. Just don't be boring," I tease.

"Hmmm...what would you like to know?"

"Tell me about your child—puphood. I don't know."

He chuckles. "I've lived in the Underworld my whole life. Hades raised me and trained me to guard the gates, and to keep the souls where they belong. There isn't much to tell." His hips rock into me, shallow movements that make my pussy quiver.

"What's your favorite color?" I ask.

"Red. You?"

"Teal. Come on, Kyon. There must be something you can tell me that doesn't require me to think," I whine.

"Oh, little flower, we have many many years for all the boring stories and factoids about me."

"Wait. Hold on. You said...fuck! You said that your knot is meant to increase the chances of pregnancy! Am I going to get pregnant now!? Why didn't you stop me? I'm too young for a pup!" My mind is reeling! My heart is hammering, and I feel a bit queasy. What am I going to do if I end up getting pregnant after only knowing this man for five seconds!?

"My heart's fire, calm down, it's okay. It isn't guaranteed that you will become pregnant with a pup. Or demon-child."

How can he be so calm!? Oh, right, he has thirteen pups, what's one more? "You don't care if I'm pregnant, do you?"

"Of course I care! If you are, we will handle that. If you're not...we will try again," he says casually, trying, and failing, to hide a smile.

"You're nuts!"

"I'm in love. You are my mate. We will be blessed with a pup of our own if the Fates deem it the right time. We will just have to...what's the saying, 'ditch that bridge when we get to it?'"

"Burn that bridge," I correct him with a huff.

He rotates his hips some more and I'm instantaneously hit with fog-brain and orgasms. Bastard. His fingers move deftly over my swollen clit and all worry and concern of being pregnant is forgotten. For now.

We are both spent and beyond the point of mobility, and the knot is still swollen enough that we can't separate. Not wanting to think about being a mother just yet, I decide to bring up the names of his other personalities.

"Let's rename Lefty and Righty then. Can I talk to them?"

"Thought you didn't want to think."

I grunt.

"Okay, fine."

Hi, petal. Lefty here. How can I help you decide on a better name?

"This is neat. Okay, umm...how are you different from Kyon?"

I am far more aggressive than he is. Quick to judge. And I'm sexier, he teases.

"So, you are a regular hot head, huh? Hmm." I run through names that fit that personality. "What do you think of Blaze?"

I love it! Boys?

Fits perfectly, Righty states.

Yeah. Definitely you, Kyon agrees.

"Ok, Blaze it is! Now... Righty? What about you?"

I am far more possessive than the others. My apologies, by the way, I'm the one that urged Kyon to claim you before you were ready. I am the take what's mine kind. More articulated than Blaze, too. He laughs uproariously.

"I'm over that," I concede. "Now...a possessive nature. That's a tough one. I'll have to think on that one for a minute. Let's see..." This one is more difficult to decide on.

"You don't *have* to think of one now," Kyon whispers, as if his other sides wouldn't hear him. I open my eyes to see him smiling devilishly.

"Nope. I need to do this. I can't give one a cool name and then leave the other hanging. That's just rude. What about Zavis? I don't know what it means, but it sounds right to me."

Zavis? Zavis. Blaze, am I a Zavis to you?

Sounds stuck up...so yeah.

Bite me. I love it, dewdrop. Thank you.

"You are most welcome! I'm glad I was able to save you from those lame ass names Kyon gave you," I say, being sure that Kyon knows I'm teasing him by kissing his chest multiple times.

I feel the pressure inside my vagina lessening as the boys tease each other over their new names. They are proud of them, though, I can tell. Zavis keeps talking in the third person so he can say it as much as possible.

Zavis likes to learn new things because Zavis is not an archaic beast.

You may not be archaic, but you are an asshole, Blaze prods. And on they go, back and forth with Kyon throwing in here and there. In all honesty, the trio remind me of a more adult version of the old men from the Muppet Show.

"There's just one more thing...or personality, we are leaving out." Forgetting about the short conversation I had with Kyon's snake tail makes me feel like a real asshole.

My mate looks at me with utter confusion. "Uh, no. There are just the three of us."

"Your snake tail. He deserves a name, too," I state.

"It's just a tail, little flower."

"I spoke with him. Are you saying you never have in all the millennia you have been living with him on your ass?"

Kyon shakes his head, looking as if I'm more on the crazy side than he thought.

He doesn't hear me. I've tried for hundreds of years before I gave up.

"He's talking in my head right now! You don't hear that?"

"Let me focus...maybe..." Kyon closes his eyes.

"Talk to me some more, snake."

I suppose it is possible with your abilities, and the mate bond, that he may finally hear me.

"There! Did you hear him?"

Shaking his head, Kyon replies, "All I hear is hissing static, little flower. Of course, that's more than I have ever heard from 'him' before."

"Well, I'm giving him a name...unless he has one?"

No, little viper, I do not have a name.

"Well, I am a bit of a Harry Potter geek...and I LOVE Snape. What do you think of that?"

"Easy to remember. I like it," Kyon says.

As do I. Thank you, little viper.

"You are most welcome, Snape. Man, I have so many pet names now from you all...I'm going to start thinking *I* have multiple personalities!" I tease, laughing against Kyon's chest.

Kyon kisses the top of my head. "I love you, little flower. You have completed me—us—in a way I never thought possible."

"I love—" I gasp, shooting up onto my elbows on his chest, our groins still linked.

"What is it? Are you hurt?" he asks, pulling up onto his own elbows. The gold of his eyes dims as he looks at me full of worry.

"No! Not at all. In fact, I am a freaking genius!" I crow. "I know who the traitor is and exactly how we are going to nail his ass!"

...to be continued...

Also by Niki Trento

The Blade's Opus
Reverse Harem Paranormal Romance

<u>Lullaby of the Sword</u>
Styx & her harem (February 2022)
<u>Sonata of the Sword</u>
Styx & her harem (TBD)
<u>Crescendo of the Sword</u>
Styx & her harem (TBD)

Seasons of the Wolf
MF Paranormal Romance

<u>Summer of the Alpha</u>
Barin and Celeste (released August 2020)

<u>Autumn of the Beta</u>
Donovan and Kathleen (released October 2020)

<u>All Axel's Eve</u>
Short Story featuring Axel and the Pups (released October 2020)

<u>Taming Kane</u>
Kane and Samson [MMF] (released January 2021)

<u>Winter of the Delta</u>
Axel and Zinnia (released March 2021)

<u>Spring of the Omega</u>
Cash and Pandora (released May 2021)

<u>Season's End</u>
The Twins (released July 2021)

Mark of the Pride
Reverse Harem Paranormal Romance

<u>Ascension of the Queen</u>
Soleil & her harem (released December 2021)
<u>Claiming the Courier</u>
Cassia & her harem (TBD)

About the Author

Niki Trento lives happily in Ohio with her husband,
daughter, and son. She is almost always seen with her seven-month-old Shollie puppy,
Cerberus.

In addition to writing, Niki enjoys photography, painting,
and almost any other craft she can get her hands on. She also loves to read and
watch Christmas movies. If they can make her cry, bonus! Niki is also team Marvel
and wishes to go hunting with Sam & Dean Winchester.

Stalk Me

Follow me on Facebook for updates on releases and other works

https://www.facebook.com/NikiTrentoAuthor

Or join my Facebook group at:

https://www.facebook.com/groups/silverlakeshifters/

You can find me almost anywhere:

linktr.ee/nikitrentoauthor

Made in the USA
Middletown, DE
15 August 2022

70605348R00086